THE TWO WARS OF JIMMY D'AUBIN

JAMES D. WILSON

ABOUT THE AUTHOR

James Wilson is a retired administrator who has worked in communications, local government and health. He is interested in history and the way it has affected society, but particularly the part his family has played in it and the societal issues they were involved in which mirror the experiences of ordinary people.

The story behind *The Two Wars of Jimmy D'Aubin* had been on his mind for several years until he finally set about writing it.

James also writes poetry and short stories and is currently working on another novel. He also paints for recreation.

Beyond his artistic endeavours James is interested in the stewardship of our environment, sustainability, renewable energy, gardening and permaculture.

He lives on a small property in Gippsland in Victoria's Strzelecki Ranges.

He is currently working on a second novel.

To My Father

ACKNOWLEDGEMENTS

Thanks to all at Sid Harta Publications for bringing this book to fruition. And a special shout-out to my editor, Tony Berry. As a first-time author I found his skill and expertise invaluable and a great help towards completing a second novel in a different and more descriptive style. Thanks to Luke Harris of Working Type Design for the great cover, it really helps to tell the story.

CONTENTS

CHAPTER 1

INTRODUCING JIMMY D'AUBIN

Jimmy D'Aubin was a bastard.

His parents, Edward and Mary, came from traditional families and followed Presbyterian teachings. One balmy Queensland Sunday afternoon after church, and during a picnic on the banks of the river, the young couple got talking and drifted away from the picnic crowd to a more secluded location with softer grass and screening scrub.

Talking turned to touching and, with surging desires, God was quickly forgotten amid the fumbling. The mechanics of it all seemed pretty straightforward to them as they had been raised on the farm and had grown up with the knowledge of animals and their beastly habits.

Anyway, they enjoyed the moment, cleaned themselves up

and rejoined the picnic crowd, continuing to keep the Sabbath holy.

From then on Sundays for Edward and Mary meant much slipping away after sermons on the sins of the flesh. After about three months it was apparent that Mary was with child and that Jimmy's journey had begun. There was much disputation between the families about what should happen so a wedding wasn't organised until a month after Jimmy was born. A private wedding was held at Mary's parents' house with necessary witnesses so that at least the law of man was satisfied.

When Jimmy was born he had very little hair, his blue eyes were wide open and he was fair skinned. He was the first of a number of boys Edward and Mary would have in creating their family, albeit those after Jimmy, in a more planned way.

Edward and Mary were farmers who found Queensland too hot and battles with the prickly pear and arsenic used to kill the vindictive plants too arduous. Their families had been lured to the outback with cheap land which the Government decided would be a good way to control the prickly pear and boost pastoral expansion. Although it seemed like a good policy it was ineffective in controlling the invasive cactus which wouldn't be beaten until the cactoblastis moth was introduced some years later. Many settlers gave up and those who stayed became as poisoned as the plants and died long slow deaths from arsenic poisoning.

Edward and Mary decided to relocate to Melbourne. By now, at the start of the twentieth century, it had become a well-established city and Victoria was the seat of the family's origin in Australia. Edward bought a butcher's shop in suburban Hawthorn and Mary kept the house in a pleasant tree-lined street not far away. As she arrived with a prefabricated family no-one knew of her shame before God and she was mostly able to push it away. Edward put a big sign on the front of the shop in Glenferrie Road which had been prepared by a signwriter and read 'Edward D'Aubin and Sons — Butchers'.

The shop was a commercial success and Edward saw no reason his sons couldn't be brought into the business in one way or another as time went on. In the meantime he sent them to the nearby Presley College so they would have the benefit of a good education, solid social standing and a light touch by God.

As Edward and Mary continued to produce boys and their marriage went from strength to strength, they became well-off and a well-respected family in the local business, church and school communities. Mary developed a circle of friendship with other women of a similar status and undertook the odd bit of charity work to assist those less fortunate, but not enough to become contaminated by it.

Jimmy grew up in the usual way for boys of the time with all the trials and tribulations that entails. He had the benefit of a private school education and an element of privilege that goes with that. Jimmy was slightly older than his brothers as a result of his parents taking a break in child production after his arrival. Jimmy helped his father in the shop after school, on weekends and during school term breaks. The work kept Jimmy well grounded and he became experienced in breaking animals down into edible products, eviscerating them, cutting through the bones, slicing the meat, making sausages and mincing up the lesser cuts. The sight of blood didn't worry him but he knew many of his school friends and others didn't like it. Maybe he would be a butcher after all and continue the family business.

He was somewhat dreamy, but serious, and while he was good at working in the shop and at ease with the customers he liked to get outside and explore the natural world. He joined the Scouts and often went on camping trips. Sometimes he thought he might enjoy a life of catching lizards and watching the tadpoles and fish in the local creek. It wasn't far to the Yarra River and occasionally he would catch a decent size fish and bring it home for his mother to cook, which she was more than happy to do — 'makes a change from meat' she would say.

At school Jimmy was interested in science and new developments, especially telephony. He was fascinated with the idea that a signal, words, music and the human voice could be transmitted and be received at another location exactly as it left. Jimmy thought it was a special magic, but plenty of people considered it a gimmick that would never amount to much.

Edward sensed Jimmy's restlessness with meat work and privately conceded that the boy would never commit to working with him on a regular or permanent basis and might find some other career. Jimmy was intelligent and keen to engage with the world so looked likely to have a good future in whatever he chose to do.

Jimmy's parents were keen for him to finish school, maybe go to university as they could afford to support him, or help him undertake some other career. Jimmy was also thinking about his future. He was now sixteen years of age and had eighteen months of school to complete. Everything was good in the D'Aubin family. Their world seemed to be comfortably drifting along in a predictable way and Jimmy had great prospects and opportunities.

While the D'Aubins' life in Hawthorn glided by, the machinations of the great powers in Europe produced an environment of escalating tension that was moving inevitably towards confrontation. There was the usual polarisation of views between people who thought war would be a good thing and a method of solving problems, those who disagreed and those who didn't know or care. In any case events proceeded and came to a head and people they previously didn't know much about quickly became their enemies.

The well-ordered worlds of Hawthorn and Presley College suddenly changed when the newspaper headline of the day announced, *Britain At War With Germany.*

What did that mean?

What did that mean for Jimmy and his family?

The customers still came into the butcher's shop and Jimmy still went to school.

From Hawthorn the view initially was blurry, distant, the implications unclear and of little consequence. As 1914 passed, the manoeuvres, particularly of the British, French and Germans, became well known and the analysis was endless. It was obvious that the war would not be over quickly and that a huge effort by the British Empire would be required.

Many Presley old boys and current students rushed off to enlist in the newly raised Australian Imperial Force (AIF). Some even sailed to England and enlisted in the British forces as they didn't want to miss out on the chance of a lifetime; they wanted to travel to distant lands to seek glory and adventure. Death, it seemed, wasn't to be an option. The school supported the old boys and many valedictory dinners and patriotic fund-raising events were held at which the principal, parents and local dignitaries made rousing speeches before the boys went off to war.

Some of the girls the boys knew also made the supreme sacrifice on the last night they were together. As a consequence a new cohort of bastards was born nine months later — about the same time the old boys were having their mangled corpses strewn across the scrubby cliffs and gullies of Gallipoli, drying in the Mediterranean sun to feed the ants and never to return.

It had all seemed like such fun until the casualty lists were posted and the names of the old boys were read out in chapel.

Jimmy was caught up in the patriotism and wanted to join the AIF as soon as he could. His parents were absolutely against it and urged him to finish school. In the end, to prevent him running away and joining up, they did a deal with him — if he completed his schooling they would sign the papers as minors below the age of eighteen could join up only with parental permission. Jimmy would finish school and turn eighteen early in 1916. His parents didn't think the war would last that long so saw no prospect of Jimmy getting to go away anyway.

The year 1914 dragged on for Jimmy. He keenly read the newspapers and saw all the pictures of units being raised, trained and shipped overseas. He longed to join up and not miss out on the adventure. He saw the pictures of the Dardanelles landing, the digging in and the fighting at places such as Lone Pine and the Nek and dreamt of being there. He saw the Anzacs sail away from Turkey after eight months and head for France for a crack at the real enemy — the Germans. He read about the heroic French, trench warfare, artillery, wire, mud and destruction.

He read about the British and Australians and their gallantry, Albert Jacka and his Victoria Cross and the next 'Big Push'. He received occasional letters from friends who were overseas who urged him to come over to help chase the Hun. He couldn't wait to go and play his part. It would be the adventure of a lifetime.

CHAPTER 2

THE CALEDONIANS

Each day Jimmy dutifully went to school, dreaming on the tram up Glenferrie Road, listening to the cicadas singing in the trees as the last part of his schooling drew to a close. He kept working in the butcher's shop, with every chop of the cleaver imagining some mortal injury he was inflicting on the enemy; carcasses were no longer sheep or cattle — they were Germans and they deserved what they got. He would show the sausage eaters a thing or two.

He finally finished school in December 1915 and turned eighteen in January 1916 and rather than get his father to sign the papers he wanted to do it himself.

Edward D'Aubin and his wife knew what was coming and they had hoped that either Jimmy would have changed his mind by now or the war would be over and they could all get on with their lives. Jimmy was a likeable, well-educated and handsome young man with the world at his feet and had plenty of opportunities for a career or further study.

His parents agreed that Edward would have a talk with the boy and try to convince him to reconsider his decision to enlist. Edward had seen the casualty lists and understood the reality of war. He had seen the grief of some of his friends whose sons had been killed overseas or returned maimed or hollowed out. He didn't want this for his son.

He had the talk.

It made no difference.

The following Saturday morning Edward went with Jimmy to Hawthorn town hall, stood in line and watched his son sign the fateful papers. He knew the boy was going to war one way or the other and, although he didn't like it, he thought this was the best way to do it. Mary was distraught and cried for a week; she never accepted that her son was going to be a soldier. Jimmy, of course, was elated.

The local unit, the Caledonian Regiment, was incorporated in the new 5th Battalion, which was part of the Second Brigade of the First Australian Division. His mother was Scottish, so joining the Caledonians made sense to him. The school cadets, of which Jimmy was a member, had been affiliated with the regiment too. He also knew many of the old boys and others in the battalion so he felt he would be with family in a sense.

Initial training was undertaken at the Broadmeadows military camp to the west of Melbourne. This was the main training base for the army in Victoria and at any one time a range of units would be training there. The recruits were mixed in together as training battalions and after training were posted as individuals to their nominal units.

In January 1916 Jimmy said goodbye to his parents and brothers and headed off to camp. His mother cried, although she hoped to see Jimmy again when his training was finished and before he embarked. She was consoled a little by feelings of patriotism, but her maternal feelings were still strong and not easily subdued.

To get to the camp Jimmy caught the train at Hawthorn into the city to Flinders Street where he changed trains for Broadmeadows, only a dozen stops or so further on. As the 'red rattler' clattered along on that hot summer afternoon with its doors open, the passengers felt the cool air and the odd grasshopper or lump of soot passing over them as they settled deep in the leather and horsehair seats. As the train travelled through the suburbs Jimmy looked out into back yards behind corrugated iron fences, the clothes lines, the fruit trees and the barking dogs. He wondered what people were doing inside the houses, what their lives were like and what they thought about the noisy train rumbling by on a regular basis. He couldn't know the answers but that didn't stop him enjoying his comfortable sleepy musing.

Gradually the suburbs gave way to more open country and shortly the train pulled up at Broadmeadows.

He saw several young men like him had got off the train,

some in uniform, some not. Many seemed to know what to do and started walking up the road bearing the sign 'Broadmeadows Military Camp, 2 miles'. He followed their example and the sign, eventually arriving at the camp covered in a film of dust from mounted troops that galloped by.

The Broadmeadows camp was huge and located on the relatively flat lands in the rural area north of Melbourne. The site was previously a grazing property and still had a scattered covering of eucalypt trees and pine windbreaks that provided some shade for those lucky enough to have their tents located under one. The surrounding country was dry and hot in summer with temperatures regularly rising to 100 degrees Fahrenheit. A large number of horses were stabled on the site as they were the main source of transport and some of the Light Horse units were also being trained there. The horses were kept clean and their stables regularly mucked out, which meant tents located downwind of them were not anyone's preferred choice.

A barbed wire perimeter fence enclosed the camp to keep the public out and the men in. The fence was continuously patrolled to ensure security, but inevitable border transgressions kept the military police busy. With all the continual troop and horse movement the site was forever full of dust that covered everything including tents, men, bedding, food and water. There were also plenty of flies and mosquitoes to add to the unpleasantness.

Jimmy reported to the guard house at the front gate and

was herded up with other new recruits while they waited for something to happen. An officer arrived and organised them into very rough ranks, aware that they were all new to the military. Following his order the men shuffled off to their barracks.

Barracks was probably too grand a word for the accommodation that consisted of a cluster of weatherboard buildings which housed latrines and mess halls for kitchens and eating. The majority of the men were housed in tents allocated by the officer as they marched past the dusty canvas. Each tent had six men allocated to it and the recruits quickly memorised the 'address' so they could find their new temporary home later. They deposited the few things they had brought with them and rejoined the marching group.

When everyone had identified their new home they were marched to a mess hall for their first army meal, gratefully received after their long day. Army food varied in quantity and quality depending on where the troops were, what they were doing and the availability of supply. In battle, enemy activity had a huge influence on when and what men could eat; a hot meal was really treasured. The meals in the camp were generally good with corned beef and cabbage something of a specialty, although the 'rat shit' garnish generally found little favour.

After their meal, the men dispersed to their tents for the evening which had cooled from the heat of the day and was now much more comfortable. They played cards, talked and got to know each other. Of those in Jimmy's tent he was most comfortable talking to a young man called Billy Carrick. They were the same age and seemed to get on pretty well. Billy was also from Hawthorn but Jimmy hadn't come across him until now.

Billy was taller than Jimmy, about six foot and with a stronger build. He was full of confidence and couldn't wait to get to France to do his bit. His father was a mechanic and had a job at the Hawthorn tram depot working on the new electric trams. Billy had a brother, and a sister a year younger than Billy, a detail that piqued Jimmy's interest. As time went by Billy and Jimmy became good friends and tended to spend any leave together.

After their first restless night in camp the men were woken by the dawn light creeping in between the tent flaps and the bird songs of magpies and kookaburras drifting across the camp. Other troops were already up and on the move. The new recruits presented to the mess hall for breakfast, were put through more marching and drilling and in the afternoon marched to the quartermaster's store for issuing of their uniform. Each received boots, shirts and trousers, tunic, hat and a range of equipment that was now their responsibility to look after on the pain of death should they lose any of it. The clothing was mass-produced and took little account of the assorted shapes and sizes of the men; it required plenty of trying on and swapping between them to find the best fit.

*

In the following days Jimmy and his colleagues were put through more marching and drills covering physical fitness, infantry tactics, weapons, enemy tactics, trench warfare, wire cutting, hygiene and much more. They now realised they were engaged in an enterprise of extreme gravity. Concentrating on their training would ultimately help them stay alive, the more tricks they could learn the better their chances of survival.

Jimmy enjoyed the weapons training and shooting practice on the rifle range best, despite the bruised arm he always suffered after each shoot. Their main weapon was the short magazine Lee Enfield .303 (SMLE) rifle, known to the troops simply as a 'three-o-three'. The rifle was heavy, clad in wood, and became a complete weapon when a bayonet was fitted at the muzzle. They also had a chance to throw a Mills bomb as these were often used in the trenches. Billy also enjoyed the weapons training, knowing that as the days went by, they were all closer to heading overseas.

When their training had finished, the men were posted to their final units. They were able to make a request for posting but the army made the final decision. Billy was posted as an infantry reinforcement to the 5th Battalion as a rifleman, Jimmy also wanted to go to the 5th and luckily, because of his knowledge and aptitude for telephony and communications, he was posted as a runner with the battalion's signals unit.

At the end of the training the men were given two days' embarkation leave. Jimmy and Billy used theirs wisely, returning home to be stuffed with food by their mothers.

They told their families about their training and tried to reassure them about the future, which proved useless when it came to boarding the ship at Railway Pier on 1 May 1916 when Jimmy's mother was inconsolable. His father was also upset but secretly, and not so secretly, proud of his son heading off to war. His excited brothers pressed Jimmy to send them a German helmet when he got to France.

The men clambered up the gangplank with their heavy packs and equipment and lined the deck to wave goodbye to their families. Their ship, the *Mercury*, gradually moved away from the dock with the streamers stretching and then breaking like some of the sets of hearts watching the departure. They steamed up the Bay, ploughed through the Heads and entered the ocean headed for France via the Suez Canal, eventually landing at Marseille in France.

CHAPTER 3

PAS DE PROBLÈME

After the ship had passed through the Heads it gradually steamed west and set course for Fremantle; there it docked briefly to take on fuel, water and stores before heading across the Indian Ocean towards Suez. While in port the troops were confined to the ship as the commanders were concerned that if they were allowed off they would be difficult to round up again and the ship couldn't wait.

The ship left Fremantle as part of a small convoy of troop and supply ships with a destroyer escort and started the most dangerous part of the trip across the very open ocean. German raiders had been operating in the area and ships had been sunk. The captain posted extra watches to scan the horizon and at night all external lighting was extinguished.

The men found the trip incredibly boring and the officers

tried to keep them busy with training, physical fitness, limited drilling and equipment exercises. There were also games and the men played cards among themselves, smoked and rested. There was an element of excitement knowing that they were off to war but exactly where they were going, when and what they would do when they got there was unknown, by the men at least due to the need for secrecy of troop movements. It was however an open secret that they were headed for France and the men easily deduced that they would be traversing the Suez to get there.

They settled into an established rhythm and routine of activities. Looking back in years to come the men remembered this as a time of great comfort. Their free time was spent writing letters to loved ones at home, walking the deck, watching the wake of the ship and occasionally sighting seabirds. Sometimes an albatross circled the ship, watching the men with their intelligent eyes and the men watching them in return, neither knowing what the other was doing or where they were going. Each continued on their way, the men to war and the albatross on its never-ending patrols.

After the long voyage across nothing but ocean they eventually sighted the coasts of Africa and Arabia, an amazing experience as most of the men had never been at sea before let alone travelled to foreign lands. They were even more impressed by the Suez Canal and the experience of the ship passing through the desert on a thin ribbon of water. They all mused about this incredible feat of engineering.

At Port Said the ship briefly docked for provisioning. This included fresh food for which the men were grateful after having seen none for some time. They knew they were approaching the end of their voyage and after a short cruise across the Mediterranean would be in France.

Jimmy and Billy were keen to get ashore. They had spent the last few weeks getting to know each other along with the other men who had been posted to the 5th Battalion reinforcements. All were keen to join the battalion and do what they had been trained for, get into the line and have a go at 'Fritz'.

The ship docked in Marseille and the men finally disembarked. They had hoped to be granted leave so that they could explore and play at being tourists, even briefly, but they were marched straight off the ship and on to a train. Other troops from the ship accompanied them on the train to join their units. The train's destination wasn't shared with the troops but they did seem to be heading north.

The journey took a couple of days with numerous delays when the train stopped in a siding, slowed down or stopped briefly and then suddenly took off. During these stops men would quickly hop off, stretch their legs and more quickly climb on board again, some hoisted on by their mates so they wouldn't be left behind. Card games helped to pass the time and Jimmy the dreamer looked at the unfamiliar landscape, drinking in the different sights, smells and the manmade and natural landscape. He thought the fields were so well ordered compared to Australia, neat and small with little villages peppered all along the way. People could be seen working outside and every now and then one would look up and wave to the troops, who would wave back and release a cheer.

When the train stopped at stations waiting for other trains to pass there were always local people offering goods for sale. Mostly it was fresh local food which the men bought to supplement their rations. They were not always sure what the food was as they had few clues about French cuisine. But they soon came to understand what they liked and the food vendors did a roaring trade. A few French words learnt during these exchanges would help in future transactions.

When the train reached Armentiéres the men were ordered off and promptly marched to a camp outside the town where they had a good meal and were able to rest for the night and join the battalion. Next day they familiarised themselves with the camp and began operational training with their new comrades. They were told they would be involved in an attack in the next couple of weeks. Jimmy and Billy found this exciting and sobering; it added an edge to the training.

Jimmy trained with the signal section and Billy with a rifle company. They were issued with gas masks for the first time and classes in the use of the masks were held to make sure the men understood their practicalities and when they should be used.

Jimmy learnt more about how signals worked in the line and the range of communications available, including telephony in normal conditions and the constant work to mend damaged lines, especially when in action. There was also the use of visual signals — in daytime and at night — and the use of runners, which was often the most effective but dangerous method.

Billy was instructed on current infantry tactics which often changed depending on new weapons being used by either side or successful actions using different methods to either attack or defend. Each side was always watching to see what worked best and gave better chances of survival.

The other men of the battalion had mostly been involved in the fighting at Gallipoli and were very familiar with being in action and all the horrors that this entailed. They were also nervous about the coming attack as this would be their first action in France against the Germans, who had a more formidable reputation than the Turks they had faced at Gallipoli. The Germans were well organised and skilled in trench warfare. The best tip the old hands could give was to 'keep your head down', a simple piece of advice, but in the line snipers were always watching.

The men were kept busy as the day of the attack approached. The evening before, the battalion was moved to a support position behind the front line ensuring they would be able to move quickly into the attack position. The attack was scheduled to begin at 0300 hours and was aimed at the German trenches at Pozières. An early morning attack would hopefully catch the Germans off guard — it was also easier to attack in the dark and harder to defend. The men moved to a starting point marked with tapes — the standard way of assembling before an attack.

As it was July the countryside was fairly dry and free of mud, making it much easier for the troops to move. It still took time to get into the front line from the support trenches due to 'traverses' designed to limit injury from a shell burst or the enfilading of a trench.

As they moved forward they heard the occasional explosion of incoming shells and saw the flashes of small arms fire. At 2 o'clock the sky lit up, accompanied by the massive boom of the Australian and British artillery opening its attack on the German trenches. This 'crash' bombardment continued until 3 am when it changed focus to the German support forces and allowed the 5th to occupy the hopefully destroyed German front line.

At 3 am the 5th left their trenches, 'jumped the bags' (the sandbags protecting their position), and headed for the German trenches, Billy with his company and Jimmy with a company commander as a messenger. The artillery bombardment had been reasonably successful and most of the battalion made it across no-man's land through the German barbed wire, which had been sufficiently destroyed to let them scramble through. There were some casualties from machine-guns located somewhere in the German supports.

The men quickly cleaned up the trenches, killing or capturing any remaining Germans and transferred the sandbags from the front of the old trenches to the new front. Things were going well and Jimmy was sent with a message back to the battalion headquarters to advise that the objective had been taken and that the company was digging in. In the meantime the German artillery opened fire on their old trenches and intensified their attack. The attack increased throughout the day but the Australians appeared to have held the new position, although there was no information coming back from other runners.

Jimmy was sent out to make contact with the front line to determine the battalion's position. This was going to be risky and dangerous. He waited for what appeared to be a break in the salvos and advanced from shell hole to shell hole using them as refuge as he crossed no-man's land. The constant vibration of exploding shells shook his innards something awful. *Phew! At last,* thought Jimmy as there among all the flashes and smoke he found the line.

He took a stunned look around. Everywhere were trenches almost completely destroyed by the shelling. So many men killed or wounded. The enemy shelling had been so severe that many of the men who survived had been buried in the earth and often had to be dug out by their mates more than once. Jimmy delivered his message and received one from the company commander in return.

He made his return across no-man's land without injury and reported what he had seen.

The battalion was withdrawn and relieved in the darkness that night with the Allied artillery effectively countering the German fire. While the objectives of the original attack had been achieved, the battalion's normal strength of around a thousand men had been reduced by a casualty list of 450 killed, wounded or missing. Jimmy and Billy had survived, Jimmy unscathed, and Billy buried once and suffering mild concussion. Welcome to France.

*

Following the battle, the battalion was able to rest for a few days in a back area. The lightly wounded recovered and rejoined their mates; reinforcements further bolstered its strength.

Their experience of battle changed Jimmy and Billy's view about the war and their part in it. They now realised they were part of a huge machine that seemed to have almost perpetual motion and would continue with or without them, their unit or any army.

Their focus needed to be on their own survival and that of their mates. This became the most important thing to them. What had happened to Billy was a good example; the only way soldiers could thank their mates for digging them out was by digging them out the next time they were covered in earth and cinders, or carting them off to a First Aid post or hauling them out of a slimy shell hole.

There was no doubt that the combat experience was one of bonding — lives depended on it.

*

Immediately after emerging from the front line and returning to camp, the men were overstrained, physically shaking and twitching. They were deadtired, filthy and hungry. They quickly ate a hot meal and fell asleep.

The next day they washed and searched their clothes for the lice that seemed to affect everyone, hiding in the seams of clothing and making their own raids to suck blood and retreat again. Occasionally the troops were able to have their clothes steamed to kill the rotten things. In the field, however, they had to search their own clothes and squash the creatures on each other when they could.

Another day passed and the men were granted twenty-four hours' leave.

They played cards, wrote letters home or simply rested. Jimmy and Billy took the opportunity to explore the nearby town and had lunch at a local estaminet. It was all so pleasant and normal — an experience they had not had for a long time.

They ordered a meal and Billy suggested that they have a beer to go with it. Jimmy had never had a drink before as his parents were strict about alcohol and his mother would not have it in the house. This was a new experience. Jimmy sipped the beer. At first taste he found it rather bitter, but after the second sip he decided that he liked it.

Many other soldiers were in town, including some of their mates who had joined them in the estaminet. The Australians were well paid compared to troops from other nations and the

French were always keen to have them on the premises as they were good for business. The drinking continued throughout, greatly helping the men to relax and unwind after their recent battlefield experience.

As the afternoon continued into the evening many of the men became quite drunk, including Jimmy, a lad not at all used to alcohol. One of the older soldiers, Albert Poath, also a signaller, told Jimmy that he and some others were heading back to camp and asked if Jimmy wanted to come too.

Jimmy declined. 'Thanks, mate, having too much fun here.' Albert and the others left without him.

About this time a group of pretty, young and some not so young or pretty women arrived and started talking to the men. The women spoke in broken English and the men responded in broken French and it soon became obvious that there was another language in which they were all fluent. The men who were 'interested' retired to back rooms where comfort services were provided and both parties rejoiced in the transaction. In his drunken state Jimmy felt he too would like to go out the back. So he chose a woman and forgot about the war for a while. He had not been with a woman before, but what he lacked in experience the woman more than made up for and the service was successfully completed.

Billy also explored the delights of the back room and they stumbled back to camp in the darkness. Both had to stop along the way to relieve themselves and in Jimmy's case also a huge spew that included his lovely lunch. Next day Jimmy awoke feeling terrible and had to endure his first hangover. He swore he would never drink again.

*

For Jimmy and Billy the war continued for more than another year with men joining and leaving the battalion for various reasons, some dead, some wounded, some prisoners, some missing — which really meant being blown to bits — and others with illness, including the dreaded venereal disease.

They were lucky to escape being seriously wounded and became fatalistic about what would happen to them as the war insidiously chipped away at their sanity. Every time they were in action, they knew it was madness and their chances of surviving another battle seemed to reduce. All that kept them going was their mates and the thought of getting home either from a significant wound or the end of the war.

After every battle when leave was granted, they went on a bit of a bender with their mates as often as they could. There were many nights of drinking and dubious entertainment, but at the time this was what kept the men going and that was good enough.

The battalion's battle honours during this time included Bullecourt, Somme, Ypres, Menin Road, Polygon Wood, Hazebrouck and others. Some of the fighting was in France and some in Belgium. Each place etched its particular horrors on the men's minds and it seemed like it would never end.

They were always haunted by a return to somewhere they had been before or a place that had a reputation.

The name of the battles provided a clue. For ease of reference, each battle was named after the place where it occurred and if a place was attacked more than once it was given a number. Thus the battalion fought at Second Bullecourt and at the Third Battle of Ypres.

And then there was Passchendaele.

CHAPTER 4

SCHRAPNELL UND GELBKREUZ

It was late 1917 in northern France and Belgium. The weather was getting colder, there was another big push aimed at dislodging the Germans in Flanders to the east of Ypres and numerous actions in which the Australians in general and the battalion in particular were involved.

The ground had been fought over and churned up by earlier battles. It was littered with shell holes, belts of rusty and fresh barbed wire, rotting bodies of men and horses, smashed equipment, trenches, tracks, stumps and shards of trees — and mud.

And then it started to rain.

The rain was incessant. So much water poured into the shell holes that wide tracts of the battlefield looked like an overlapping fabric of ponds. Bomb craters were filled with dirty, slimy, festering mud that was stirred up every time a shell landed in the vicinity. The troops lined the tracks with duckboards so the men could make their way across the blasted landscape. While the wooden boards helped spread the weight across the ooze, they became treacherously slippery with the mud from the boots of hundreds of feet and the never-ending rain. It was so easy to slip off the tracks and into deeper mud or a shell hole. The men were not only encumbered with all their equipment but were also required to carry extra supplies such as ammunition, tools and food further forward for themselves or other troops. Weighed down by these loads many men slipped off the tracks and into the mud. Unfortunately some could not be reached and it was not unknown for them to drown in the morass, never to be seen again.

When not in the front line the troops were usually expected to undertake a range of other necessary works. At this time Jimmy and his unit were helping divisional signals bury telephone lines to protect them from damage.

Jimmy knew it was preferable to bury the lines rather than have to repair them or spool out new wire under fire as he had lost many 'liney' mates and had endured plenty of close calls himself. As they were some distance from the front line they were relatively safe from immediate attack. However the Germans occasionally sent a shell in their direction, causing them to scurry for cover and temporarily stop work.

What are they up to now? Jimmy wondered. *Is it random shelling or are they registering their guns for range and location ahead of an attack? And is it imminent or some days away? Can't work them out.*

Regardless of the answer, Jimmy and his mates kept digging the slop, which slumped back into the channel almost as soon as they shifted it and buried the phone lines as fast as they could. It was cold, difficult work but they kept going, stopping only to scrape the mud off their boots with their shovels as it gradually thickened on the soles and added weight, making it difficult to walk. They were issued with waterproof capes which were meant to keep them dry, but with the wind and the work they were wet through for days on end. One hot meal a day was brought up to them, but it was usually cold by the time it got there thanks to the notoriously slow journey on the duckboards. It could take half a day to travel a mile or two due to mud, congestion and shelling.

Although not on the front line, the men were still well forward and the treacherous conditions meant they were unable to make it back to the rear for shelter. So they camped or carved out their 'pozzies' in any higher ground or old trenches in the vicinity. Otherwise, they were out in the open. To some extent it didn't seem to matter what they did; they were cold, covered in mud, wet and tired. They were exhausted when their shift had finished and just fell and slept where they were, waking only when a grimy hand on their shoulder forced them to stir. The experienced men were used to this and the rare shell didn't worry them.

The Germans were aware that the Allies were preparing

for an attack against the low Passchendaele ridge and could see the increased activity of the troops preparing in the lower lands below. To disrupt the preparations they shelled the support areas, a standard procedure to dislocate offensive actions.

The evening started quietly enough with the Germans putting up magnesium parachute flares to help them see what was happening as much of the preparation occurred at night under the cover of darkness. The trick was to keep as still as possible because any movement tended to at least attract the heavy machine-guns and maybe the occasional shell.

The word among the troops was that if you heard a shell you were usually going to be all right; it was the one that you didn't hear that had your name on it. Which was far too true in Jimmy's case. He was deep asleep and heard not a sound from the one that got him as the Germans hit their position with a crash bombardment.

He felt the force of the shell, the pressure, the flash, a deafening sound and the concussion.

He was blown out of his trench and scudded across the muddy ground towards the lip of another shell crater, losing his equipment, tin hat and jacket in the blast. He fell unconscious before the pain hit him.

In order to wreak maximum damage the Germans used a variety of shells. The men left after that initial shelling now heard the slightly different sound of gas shells incoming and landing. They pulled on their gas masks as quickly as they could in the darkness and rain. As always, some didn't make it in time.

Gradually the shelling ceased and there was an opportunity to attend to the casualties and get them to the rear. It was hard to locate everyone in the darkness and continual rain and it took them a while to find Jimmy.

After slowly regaining consciousness, he felt an intolerable burning in his lungs and eyes, and the agony of his wounds. Although badly wounded and gassed he was sure he was still alive. He heard echoey voices, Australian voices, and was aware of being handled and placed on a stretcher. He was writhing around so much that they tied him down for the stumbling journey to a First Aid post where he was given morphine for the pain and covered in a dryish, cleanish blanket.

From there, because of the conditions it took four men to carry the stretcher on the next stage. Even so, they dropped him a couple of times as they slid off the track in the darkness. Eventually they reached the Menin Road and entered Ypres, or what was left of it. The ruin of the old Cloth Hall was visible now and then by the flash of distant shellfire. They made their way to the field hospital and deposited their burden.

Hospital staff were unsure whether Jimmy would survive. He was triaged and eventually attended to, just one of dozens of casualties they had to deal with that night.

Jimmy's eyes were rinsed as best they could be, but he was suffering badly from the effects of the gas. He was still breathing but there was nothing they could do for his lungs except wipe away the bloody sputum from time to time. Lumps of shrapnel were embedded in his flesh along his left side. There was a large wound above his eye, a throat wound, a groin wound and the shrapnel had scraped the flesh off his left arm and shin and scalloped the bone along the way. Most of his left calf muscle had been blown off, his hearing was affected, he had concussion and had lost a lot of blood. He also had some skin burns as a result of the gas.

They did what they could for Jimmy, stitching up wounds with the remaining flesh and skin. After picking out most of the shrapnel, washing off the gas residue and scraping off the mud, they identified him for transport to England for further treatment if he survived the night.

As daylight crept into the tent with the rain still drumming on the canvas, the doctor declared that Jimmy would probably survive and so he was shipped off. The journey took three days and passed in a blur as he was in and out of consciousness with the pain. Not all his fellow travellers survived but Jimmy was lucky enough to arrive in England alive and receive further medical attention. His first few weeks in hospital were the same as he was continually prodded and taken off for a range of surgeries that he wasn't even aware of.

His condition eventually began to stabilise and he began to feel better as his wounds gradually healed, although the contamination from the mud, particularly for his throat wound, caused ongoing infection problems. He was still blinded from the gas and it wasn't expected that he would ever see again. At least his hearing and concussion began to improve.

Jimmy didn't know what to do, not that he was in a position to make any decisions at the moment. Questions went round and round in his mind.

What use will I be? What will I do if I can't see? He was so confused.

Billy visited him once while he was in hospital. He too had been wounded and evacuated to England although his wounds were not so serious. When they were healed Billy would be sent back to the battalion.

'Good to hear your voice, mate,' said Jimmy.

'Sorry to see you copped it so badly,' said Billy.

'Yeah, well, wrong place wrong time,' came the halting reply.

'Shell must have had your name on it, isn't that what they say?'

'Guess so, but what about you?

'Coming good, slowly,' said Billy. 'Doc reckons they'll be soon sending me back to the battalion.'

Another time Albert dropped in to see Jimmy when he was on leave in London. He brought news of how the other signallers were faring and that a couple of their mates were killed at Passchendaele.

For Jimmy, the war in Europe was over. It was time for him to go home.

CHAPTER 5

WELCOME HOME

As the routine of the hospital continued around him — the cleaning, the clanging, the cries of pain, the coughing in the night, the new arrivals, the departures for repatriation and for burial — Jimmy's wounds gradually began to heal.

The gas burns healed first then the gouges in the flesh. His lungs still gave him trouble but seemed to be getting better, allowing him to breathe more easily and with less pain. His eyes had stopped burning but he was still unable to see, although the flash of a shell burst somehow seemed to be etched on to his retina and every now and then he seemed to be able to see it. The concussion had passed and his hearing was better but he continued to have ringing in his ears.

With the improvement in his condition Jimmy was considered fit enough for travel and the prospect of returning home lifted his spirits, not that he thought he would be any use for anything; *if a man couldn't see what use was he to himself or anyone else?* Yes, Jimmy had survived, but he knew that the hospital was keen to move patients on so the bed he occupied could be filled by some other victim of war.

A hospital bed is better than lying in the cold Flanders mud or getting blown to bits. At least in here you're warm, fed, relatively safe and comfortable. That was one thought he was sure of. Jimmy did a lot of thinking … it was the one thing he could do.

In early 1918 Jimmy was allocated to a ship, the *Pegasus*, and said his goodbyes to the nurses and the doctors who had looked after him and patched him up. He was duly loaded on board with other returning soldiers. They had a range of injuries, no legs, no arms, no face, no balls, and every other missing or damaged bit in between, often in combination. Although Jimmy was blind at least he still had his eyes, others didn't even have those.

The ship steamed out of Southampton and headed for the Mediterranean via Gibraltar and on to Suez, before crossing the Indian Ocean and home.

As the ship left the Channel, Jimmy felt the swell of the North Atlantic in the wallowing of the vessel. The dank smell of England drifted away to be replaced with the salty smell of the open ocean. No more mud and wire and the noise of war and cries of men. Maybe he was now free of all that.

Most of the journey, like the outward one, was boringly mundane with mealtimes and trips to the dunny. He took every opportunity to get up on deck with the help of his crutches and other wounded men. He loved the smell of the sea and the wind in his hair, sometimes relatively gentle, sometimes gale force, which meant he had to really hang on. He didn't like being outside when it was cold or raining, he'd had enough of that for a while.

As the trip progressed there came times when he was able to sit out in the sun and absorb its life force. It was the best medicine he had found so far and was a reminder of Australia and summers past.

The other men told him what was happening, where they were and of other things he couldn't see. Bulletins were posted daily and they read those to him too. For some of the men, while their war was over, the trip became too much for their bodies and they lost their personal battles. Most went in the night, leaving their bunkmates to notice their passing in the morning. For reasons of hygiene the funerals were held as soon as possible and there were many days following the sombre ceremonies when the coffins slid over the side and the records were endorsed: 'Died at sea'. Jimmy didn't know all the dead men, but he went to the ceremonies as a duty, knowing that it was a fate he had only just escaped and he was grateful for this.

The storms and the quiet times at sea passed and the ship reached Fremantle, dropping off injured soldiers from Western Australia. The next port was Adelaide, where the process was repeated, and finally for Jimmy, they were in Melbourne.

The *Pegasus* entered Port Phillip Heads, steamed up the

bay with its damaged cargo and docked in Port Melbourne to unload the men. The next of kin had been advised which ships men were being transported on and anticipated the arrival dates. Anxious relatives keenly watched the newspapers where updated information was published. As a result most of the relatives that could be or wanted to be, were on the pier to meet the soldiers upon their return.

Jimmy's parents knew of his wounds and were there to greet him. Plenty of others were also there to meet their loved ones or what was left of them. There were also a few absentees as some wives, girlfriends and others had decided that they had no use for crippled, blind or mad men, and these men were left to find their own way home or some other place to be cared for. Some of them never made it home again and it was not uncommon for them to build a humpy down by a river or out in the bush to live by themselves with the horrors and to shun others and be shunned. People knew about the strange men living in these places, "a returned man" they would say in hushed voices and people understood.

Edward and Mary were so glad to see Jimmy and there were plenty of tears. They didn't recognise him at first. Although he was still a young man, he now looked older from the strain. He had lost a lot of weight and his eyes and wounds were still bandaged. He walked with the aid of crutches and another man. However, his auburn hair and his voice were recognisable.

Papers relating to Jimmy's wounds and their care were sticking out of his pocket. His father took charge of them to read later. They helped him on to a train headed for Flinders Street, changed trains for Hawthorn, then hobbled him home the short distance from the station. On the trains Jimmy heard the whispers that others thought he couldn't hear.

'Look at that poor bastard,' someone said.

A stranger came up to Jimmy and forced his hand into Jimmy's undamaged right hand, trying to shake it. 'Welcome home, mate,' he said.

CHAPTER 6

BROWN SHOOTS

Jimmy was so tired. But his mother made him a cup of tea and served him up a big meal, the first supper. He ate it and it was delicious, something he hadn't really thought about. She wanted to talk to him but what could he say? His brothers were apprehensive about his appearance but were still looking for the German helmet. His father decided to leave him alone. He pulled the medical papers from his pocket, now somewhat worn and dirty. They were not very comprehensive, but factual and clinical. What concerned Edward most of all was Jimmy's vision. All the papers noted was that he was 'totally blinded by mustard gas attack at Passchendaele, minimal improvement to date, can tell night from day'.

As Mary helped Jimmy into bed, she realised she was going to have to spend a lot of time with him. All he wanted to do was sleep. Once he was asleep Mary left him and joined Edward in the 'good room'.

The other children were in bed. They spoke quietly about Jimmy, noticing that there was something different about him, although they couldn't say what. Mary thought it would be a nice surprise to have a celebratory dinner with a few friends to welcome Jimmy home, so she set about organising it.

Jimmy slept on and off for the next few days, mostly only waking to eat, his mother changing his dressings as required. She had done a dressings course in preparation for his return and was proud that she could help. They were to attend a Caulfield repatriation hospital that dealt with returned men the following week for further treatment and advice and she hoped that she would learn more then.

His brothers left him alone. They were slightly scared of him and repulsed by his injuries. His father tried to chat with Jimmy and tell him about the family and the goings on in the butcher shop. Jimmy grunted in the right places but didn't give much away.

Keep your own counsel, he told himself. *How can I tell them about the war, the things I've seen, the mates I've lost?*

He thought of things the Germans did, the things the British did, and the Australians. The pain and despair of it all. Above all, how he felt right now, his fear of the future. *Give them the bare minimum, tell them what they want to hear and let them be happy with that.*

His mother took him to Caulfield where the doctors looked

at his wounds, dressed them and mumbled knowingly and sagely from time to time. They were pleased with his progress except for the throat wound that was still giving Jimmy some pain and wasn't healing that well. It seemed to repeatedly get infected. Maybe it still had some of that Flanders mud. All they could do was keep dressing it and hope it got better.

His lungs seemed to be pretty much healed. He was breathing normally and from an army medical perspective they were no longer an issue. He was able to walk well by himself but with his low vision the continued use of crutches was still necessary.

His sight seemed to be gradually improving and he could now see moving shapes as well as fully recognising day from night. The doctor explained that the effects of the gas on eyesight was extremely variable. It depended on a range of things including the amount of gas, how long there was contact with it, and the individual. The impact of gas on large numbers of people was unknown. The doctor said some men were able to see again relatively quickly and some after a time. Some were always compromised and others were never able to see again. The doctor was hopeful that Jimmy would gain more sight based on his improvement to date, although as it was some months since the gassing any progress was likely to be slow. He found the doctors were quite good with all the injuries they could see and touch but not so much with the internal troubles.

*

It was now autumn in Melbourne and the softer sun flickered through the wisteria vines overhanging the back veranda. Jimmy would sit there on a bench his father had made for him feeling the gentle life force seeping into his broken body and gradually helping it repair itself. His mother fed him well as mothers do in the belief that it would help his recovery, and it did. He started to put on weight and feel somewhat better, and this improved his various conditions.

Mary read to him from the papers. Although this kept him up to date on happenings in the local area this didn't interest him all that much. His real interest was in news from abroad and the progress of the war. He yearned for information about the battalion and how it was going. *Are my mates and comrades still alive and what were they doing?* He received a postcard from Billy which didn't say much except that he was well and hoped the war was over soon so they could share a beer at the Falcon Hotel in Hawthorn.

Edward felt he could best help his son's recovery by supplying good quality meat from the shop and vegetables from his garden. One of Edward's passions was his vegetable garden which he lovingly tended and plastered with huge amounts of horse manure. The manuring compulsion was welcomed by the flies, and while the garden produced plenty of vegetables it also produced its fair share of flies. Tomatoes were his favourite, which he preserved and made sauce with for use when the family couldn't have them fresh.

As part of helping with Jimmy's physical rehabilitation

Mary took him shopping with her whenever she went, which was most days. They would bump into people she knew and occasionally someone Jimmy knew. They all wanted to talk to him about the heroic adventure of the war but he wanted to avoid it as he knew the truth. While they probably meant well, he couldn't stand it. Sometimes he would meet another returned man and they would exchange pleasantries, check each other's credentials, which unit, which battle, what wound. Then they grasped hands and continued on their way knowing that was enough.

His brothers kept going to Presley College school as Jimmy had done. They were a few years younger than him and so were unable to enlist, even though it was something they dreamed of doing. Jimmy was their hero and they told their friends about him, but because he wouldn't tell them what it was like and what had happened, they made it up. They wanted to enlist like he did, hopefully with the Caledonians, and head overseas. So, they hoped the war lasted long enough. The brothers were still a bit wary of Jimmy but the oldest, Boyd, who was closest to Jimmy before the war, was able to talk to him and they had long discussions on a range of safe topics such as history, politics and religion, but the war was *verboten*.

Jimmy gradually grew stronger through the winter and with further treatment at Caulfield and the ministrations of his parents he was soon able to get around by himself. His vision had improved but was still blurry at times so he needed glasses for reading. But he was able to dispose of the crutches.

The army was also pleased. It pronounced him rehabilitated and discharged him in an act Pilate would have been proud of. But this was the way it was.

Although Jimmy had saved a little money from his army pay he still needed to work. But when he tried to find a job no one was keen to take on a man who was wounded so badly and had ongoing issues. He did occasional work in the butcher's shop but he found it tiring and it wasn't sustainable, even though his father and the other staff were quite understanding. He had no strength in his left arm and couldn't lift it above shoulder height, which ruled out doing much of the manual work the job demanded.

As the war dragged on and on Jimmy was able to read reasonably well for himself how it was going. Sometimes he couldn't believe that he had been there and then he felt a shudder of pain to remind him that he had and his mind drifted back to the trenches. At such moments his mother wondered where he was and what he was thinking, but by now she knew better than to ask other than when she needed to interrupt the thought journey to get his attention. The Americans had joined the war and were starting to help the Allies prevail against the Germans. The Australians continued to fight and had some great victories and according to some historians were instrumental in winning the final battles and therefore the war.

*

After the years of grinding horror, the bleeding, the twitching of wounded flesh, the noise and the anguish of men, women, children and animals, particularly the horses, the war came to what seemed to be a sudden end.

The papers shouted that the Armistice was to come into force at 11 am on the eleventh day of November 1918. After all that had happened Jimmy was stunned, glad that it was over and that he was out of it, and glad that he might get a chance to see his mates again. His family was elated and wanted to celebrate. The community was overjoyed and there were spontaneous victory marches up Glenferrie Road. Decorated signs appeared in shop windows and all sorts of victory-branded products and victory events were organised. For Jimmy, his victory was that he had survived and he didn't care too much about all the other stuff.

He decided to walk down to the Falcon Hotel and have a beer like he used to do in France, and remember his mates and others who didn't make it. It was the first time he had been out by himself since he had returned, but he felt up to it so walked to the hotel and ordered a beer. He was far from being alone as many others were there celebrating, including a lot of returned men. The beer was flowing, especially when the publican announced, 'The beer's on the house today, and there's free lunch and dinner for all returned men.'

Jimmy didn't need any encouragement. He knocked off his first pot, then a second and his free counter lunch of fish and chips. He thought he would have another one or two and then head home. But he found the atmosphere contagious and for the first time since being back in Australia, he felt good. He encountered some men from the 5th whom he knew and some he didn't and ended up drinking with them. The afternoon dragged on and the beer kept flowing.

It was just before 6 pm when the publican called last drinks. By then the bar was full of men who had drunk too much. Jimmy was no exception. He lined up another three beers and guzzled them down as quickly as he could. He felt the room starting to spin and he knew he had to get home, fortunately only a short walk away.

Gripping the front fences to steady himself, he made it. Overstepping and stumbling, he clattered awkwardly through the front gate and onto the veranda. As he grabbed the veranda post he felt the acid rising and knew he was going to be sick. And he was.

He also needed to relieve himself, spraying most of it over the edge of the veranda and onto the wisteria. Some went over the front of his pants and sprinkled his shoes. Then he passed out. His mother found him later that evening stretched out on the veranda bench with his pants wet with urine and lumps of regurgitated semi-chewed chips down his front. He stank of spew and urine and grog.

With the assistance of Edward, Mary got his clothes off, gave him a rough wash and got him into bed.

Next day Jimmy felt terrible and more than a little crestfallen. His parents said little. They decided the end of the war didn't happen every day and Jimmy was unlikely to provide a repeat performance.

Understandably Jimmy hadn't told them about what counted for entertainment for the troops overseas. His parents were Christians and his mother was involved with the local Temperance Union, convinced that liquor was the root of all evil. She had ample proof of that on her veranda, which she had hosed down and put away the hose.

There was quiet around the dinner table for some time after that. Jimmy expressed the appropriate level of remorse and his mother in particular enjoyed the degree of power that the incident had inadvertently bestowed upon her.

*

Following the Armistice Day incident, Jimmy's physical injuries continued to mend and he became more mobile. He was getting out more but still wasn't working and continued to live with his parents which caused him plenty of frustration. He spent his days sleeping, which helped heal his body. The dreams were harsher though, the screams, the rain and mud, and always the shell flash. When he woke it took him moments to realise where he was and sometimes get out from under the bench where he had taken cover, shaking, sweating and shouting. Everyone in the house put it down to 'Jimmy's nightmares'.

The warming sun coaxed the cicadas out of the ground to climb the stems of plants and leave their old shells behind, crisply clenched around branches. They tuned their instruments by rubbing their musical bits against their bodies. A sign that summer was back again, Jimmy heard them on the wind and their deafening noise made it through the rustling wisteria enough to wake him and end the latest nightmarish instalment. He quite liked their sound and the warmth and life they implied. When woken like this he would listen for hours to their hypnotic tone.

With Christmas drawing near Jimmy was invited to various family celebrations which seemed all about duty and he couldn't wait to get away. He dearly wanted to be back with the battalion or with his mates having a beer and talking about things that only they knew about and were unable to share with others. Instead, he was trying to fit in to the unfamiliar suburban world that he had willingly left when he enlisted and to which he felt he could never return. As these gatherings were annoyingly 'dry' he wasn't able to soothe the jagged edges of his nerves, something he found he needed to do more and more.

He slipped away and headed to the Falcon for some 'medicine' and for a while felt the undulation rather than the spike. His parents tried to get him to attend church as they thought that might iron him out and help him meet decent people rather than returned men who seemed to be interested only in carousing, something of which God and society apparently did not approve.

On Christmas eve Jimmy set out for a beer at the Falcon.

It was a hot day and he watched the droplets of condensation roll down the sides of beer glasses. All around was the bustle and noise of men throwing back the beer, spilling it on the squelchy carpet, perhaps smashing the occasional glass, swearing, shouting, and there was the occasional scuffle. As 6 o'clock approached the landlord called for 'last drinks' and the crowded bar became a sea of full glasses, then of empty glasses as the men poured them down their throats as quickly as they could. Must get in as many as possible — Merry Christmas.

Jimmy felt fine on his stumble home, this time making it to bed with minimal fuss.

The next day he was nowhere near as good, but at least the bed was more comfortable than the veranda.

*

Over the next few weeks, Jimmy went out more and more, always somehow finding his way to the Falcon and the gradual establishment of a pattern of drinking and feeling better.

In February 1919 a contingent of the 5th returned home and were set to have a celebration in Brighton to mark the event. Jimmy and others caught the train down and found their way to the Central Hotel. The publican watched his profits rising as the men got stuck into the grog and the celebration grew rowdier and rowdier. The local police looked in to keep an eye on things, but soon moved on as they were hopelessly outnumbered.

Jimmy drank his fill and more and by closing time could barely stand. Eventually he made it to the door as it slammed shut behind him. He stumbled out into the street, heading for the railway station. With all that drink on board he urgently needed to relieve himself and knew he wasn't going to make it to the station. There was no alternative but to use a shop front, spattering the window much to the shock of passers-by and the shopkeeper's wife watching from inside.

Police continuing to patrol the streets of Brighton saw Jimmy spraying the shop and promptly arrested him for offensive behaviour. He was taken to the cells and locked up with others who had also offended the locals. Jimmy was to be formally charged and released in the morning. He slept fitfully amid the groans and snores of men who reeked of vomit and grog. The heavy stench was not improved by an inmate who had even lost control of his bowels. Men yelled out to be released and swore at the police, but it didn't do them any good.

When morning came the police hosed out the cells ready for the next night's intake and Jimmy was hauled to the front desk. He was charged, his fate to be decided in court. Jimmy felt terrible but somehow managed to catch the train home feeling like he was still drunk. His mother greeted him at the door. There was no hiding her anger.

'Me and your father have been up all night worrying where you were,' she told him. 'You need to mend your ways, Jimmy, or there'll be no room for you here.'

He had no answer and dropped his gaze to the ground, unable to look her in the eye.

'You're setting a bad example to your brothers and bringing disgrace to the family.'

Jimmy was in no mood or condition to respond and slunk off to bed for a proper sleep.

When he woke, he still felt poorly and was grateful that his mother was willing to prepare him a meal. As he ate, he told Edward and Mary what had happened and how he had been charged by the police, which set his mother off again.

'How do you expect me to hold my head up at church with everyone knowing my son is a drinker AND a criminal?'

His father spoke along the same lines but at least was prepared to provide support by funding a lawyer to speak on Jimmy's behalf and offer some sort of defence. Like his wife, he knew it could be bad for business if his customers knew him to be the father of a malefactor.

A summons was issued for Jimmy to appear at the next sitting of the Brighton Court of Petty Sessions where the magistrate, a Mr Grimware, listened to the police charge and Jimmy's defence. He sagely pulled at his greying beard, reviewed the gallery and spoke of community concern about returned servicemen and their liking for alcohol, and their riotous and offensive behaviour.

'Fined ten shillings for offensive behaviour,' he announced.

Jimmy reckoned he had got off lightly and really didn't care much as he thought he could get away with it. He moved away from his parents, changed his name (but not officially) to James Brownham and found some gardening work. He was able to get cheap accommodation in a boarding house, which was really just somewhere to sleep. He earned enough pay for his drinking and had a little left over for food.

Drinking became Jimmy's favourite pastime. He was arrested in Richmond for being drunk, kept overnight in the cells but released without charge. It seemed the police were too busy to deal with him this time.

Because he hadn't paid the fine imposed in Brighton the long arm of the law got to work and the police issued a warrant for Jimmy's arrest and imprisonment. The *Police Gazette* recorded that 'Jimmy D'Aubin, known also as James Brownham, is to be imprisoned for twenty-four hours for default of payment of fine of ten shillings for offensive behaviour, gardener, 5ft, 4in, fair complexion, fair to ginger curly hair, medium build, father lives in Hawthorn.'

Eventually the police caught up with Jimmy. They arrested him and took him to Pentridge prison to serve his twenty-four hours. His photo was taken, front on and side on with his hat — a Panama. He looked dazed and felt it, he didn't really know what was going on. His official record also noted that he was a painter. To the question whether he could read and write, the reply was — both.

It was all a bit of a shock, one minute a free man, the next a prisoner. Called for muster, counted, fed with all the others, it was like being in the army again. At night he was marched off to a cell with other men for an uncomfortable sleep. In the morning he was marched out into the bright daylight, dismissed and released, and escorted out through the imposing prison gates. He walked down Sydney Road towards his lodgings in Market Street, Fitzroy. It took him a while as he wasn't the fastest walker, but he got there in the end.

He had been well fed with the prison breakfast, but now he needed a drink. Jimmy was a practical man and as he had no money and no odd jobs lined up, the solution was obvious; he needed to get some. As he passed a house, he noticed that a window facing the street was open but no one appeared to be at home. He ducked inside, rummaged through the bedside tables and found a small amount of cash and jewellery. He pocketed it all.

With cash in his pocket, Jimmy headed for the Welcoming Arms. The first beer that slid down his throat made the world a bearable place and wiped away the prison experience. Sunlight flickered on the golden liquid and the bubbles rose to form a light froth; the smell of hops invaded his nostrils. He needed another one, and another. He spent the whole day drinking, pleased that he was able to fund it.

Between the beers he was able to sell the jewellery he had grabbed from the house as there were always people in the pub willing to buy stuff like that with no questions asked. The buyer particularly liked a ring Jimmy had stolen and gave him a few quid for it, cash to fund his needs for a while. The pub was also a good place to pick up tips for jobs when he felt able to work.

As closing time approached, Jimmy still had a thirst for more, so he bought a flagon of cheap red wine and headed for his room. While the Diggers in France liked their beer, many of them were also introduced to drinking French wine and Jimmy was no exception. The flagon's contents were nothing like the wine he had in France — it was harsh and industrial but cheap, and it did the job. He wasn't supposed to drink in his room. The boarding house had two rules — no alcohol and no women in the rooms. Most boarders broke one or both of the rules regularly, and joyfully the rules weren't enforced. The landlady knew most of her customers wouldn't care about the rules and she was realistic about it.

Jimmy climbed the stairs to his room and got stuck into the flagon. It was rough but soothing, and helped transition into the night as the sun went down. Eventually, Jimmy had to make a dash to the permanently filthy communal toilet with excrement stuck to the back of the porcelain, floating turds and soggy toilet paper. The floor was slippery with urine and chunked with the occasional vomit.

Jimmy swayed and aimed as best he could, urine jetting all over the seat and the floor, dribbling down his already dirty, stained trousers, but he felt the physical relief. While he had made it to the toilet this time, often he didn't and there were many scungy stained patches on the worn floor covering that once must have been a carpet. When he was finished, he made it back to his room where he drank more of the plonk before passing out.

Tomorrow was another day, he was cashed up, he had served his time in prison and things were looking up.

While Jimmy's immediate need for resources seemed to be solved, unfortunately for him he was seen entering the house he had robbed and the neighbour who saw him was able to give a very good description to the police. The police also had informers in the pubs and one of them was able to pass on information on Jimmy's misdeeds.

He was subsequently arrested and charged with larceny. He was brought before the magistrate at Hawthorn who noted his previous conviction and sentenced him to three months with hard labour.

It was back to Pentridge again for Jimmy.

CHAPTER 7

BLUESTONE COLLEGE

Pentridge was old and constructed out of bluestone, a very hard volcanic rock, presumably so that inmates who might try their luck at escaping would have a mammoth task dislodging a block or scraping or cutting it.

There were escapes from the gaol but none through the bluestone blocks. It was the main gaol in Victoria and had accommodation for a range of criminals from the mild to the murderous. From time to time it saw the hanging of some of the latter; the bodies were quickly buried in unconsecrated ground and covered in quicklime — best that their earthly remains be eliminated as quickly as possible.

Jimmy went through the usual admission procedures he had experienced for his earlier overnight stay, so he well understood what was happening. This time, however, they found a single cell for him, a room of his own you might say. Space for a hard bed, a blanket and a bucket. Not much, but probably more comfortable than other places he had or hadn't slept in over the last few years. He spent lots of time in the cell, except for meals or when he was working.

As he was a low-risk prisoner and not imprisoned for crimes against the person, he was permitted to eat meals in the prisoners' eating area. To call it a dining room would be too grand. Like Pentridge itself, it was basic but practical; community and prison policy made sure life was not too comfortable for prisoners, with all these minor discomforts considered part of their punishment. These men had done bad things and they were supposed to suffer for it.

The gaol ran a number of industries to fulfil the requirements of hard labour and Jimmy was assigned to the factory that manufactured wire netting. When he committed misdemeanours — which was not difficult to do considering all the rules and regulations — he was given a cold chisel and hammer and set to breaking rocks in the prison yard with other unfortunates.

Jimmy had a laugh to himself. *How bloody ridiculous when I think of some of the misdemeanours me and Billy got up to in France. All those times we went AWOL and the officers let us off because they knew that booze, women or both were involved.*

Everyone knew the officers were up to the same things themselves whenever they got the chance.

Working in the wire factory and chip, chip, chipping away at rocks, taking meals, time alone in his cell became a routine that soon passed and Jimmy completed his three-month sentence.

He looked back at the prison gates on the second of January and made a silent vow: *Goodbye, Pentridge, and good riddance. You won't be seeing me again.*

He returned to his old lodgings where he was able to get a room again. The landlady knew where he had been and for how long, so she had kept his possessions for him: one old and holey, dirty blanket and a few clothes. Any other old stuff he had left with his parents and didn't really care about.

That same afternoon he returned to his old watering hole at the River Clyde Hotel in Carlton to celebrate his release. He didn't have much money owing to his recent indisposition but enough to get a few beers in. He felt much better for that and between the beers and the burps forgot about prison and his injuries for a while. He asked around the other drinkers, some of whom were casual drinkers and some full time, about the prospects for any work. Finding employment was always difficult for Jimmy because of his physical condition but now it was even worse because he had done time.

Someone flicked a soggy beer mat at him bearing a Fitzroy address written in pencil and suggested he front round there in the morning. There was some painting work available. Jimmy was grateful for the tip, finished his last beer, went back to his lodgings and slept off the beer so he was bright and fresh in the morning.

He turned up at the house and picked up a few days' work,

not much but enough for a few days drinking. Fortunately the man who ran the painting job liked his work. Jimmy was slow but good and he was retained for when his skills were needed. This suited Jimmy as it allowed time for other activities, principally holding up the bar at the River Clyde. Work was good when it was available and provided Jimmy with enough to pay his board with some left over for a drink.

But it wasn't really enough to fully fund his needs.

Having plenty of spare time, Jimmy was able to stake out houses and work out when they were and weren't attended with a view to breaking in and relieving the owners of their valuables. The regularity of this activity was driven by his need for cash; he was able to sell the stolen items around the pubs or at the pawnbroker. Inevitably, his rather amateur activities didn't go unnoticed for long. He was again arrested by the police and this time appeared at the Melbourne General Sessions. In October 1920 he was sentenced to twelve months' hard labour on each of two counts of larceny and housebreaking with intent, and ordered to be detained in a reformatory prison at the Governor's pleasure. During sentencing the magistrate commented on Jimmy's 'supposed withered arm' and that he had two previous convictions.

Jimmy was loaded into a prison van and sent to the reformatory prison, Pentridge. Back again. More wire and more rocks.

*

Over the next year or so Jimmy was moved around the prison system and served time at Melbourne Gaol, Pentridge Prison, Pentridge Reformatory Prison and Castlemaine Reformatory Prison. His health was never good and he was admitted for some months to the Castlemaine Hospital and Melbourne Hospital.

It was then decided that he needed an operation. This was performed at Melbourne Hospital after which he was released on parole for the remainder of his sentence. He received a skin graft for his throat wound which had been getting infected and causing him a great deal of pain.

He still had difficulty swallowing and because he faced a significant recovery time he moved back home with his parents for a while. Mary continually sniffed around him for the scent of alcohol. From time to time he couldn't but help disappointing her. Nor could she hold her tongue and had no hesitation in letting him know what she thought.

He knew he had to leave as soon as he was feeling better. Despite her tongue lashings her care was good and much appreciated by Jimmy. But he grew sick of the nagging and knew he would continue to have a life very different from that of his parents.

*

The boarding house beckoned and Jimmy returned, the landlady surprised to see him again because he had been away for so long. She didn't care as long as he paid the rent. She knew his money was as good as that of any other boarders no matter where it came from. She was well aware where it came from and accepted that she and her boarding house depended on the wrongdoings of others. It kept the wolf from the door.

Back at the River Clyde Jimmy tried to find more work but it was difficult as ever and he slipped back to the tried and true way of raising funds, breaking into houses, stealing, converting goods to cash in dingy, smoky pubs and sleazy pawnbrokers who knew him. The buyers didn't give him much for his goods, they knew where and how he obtained them and that he was desperate for a quid.

As for Jimmy, he knew his freedom was in their hands so he didn't argue too much about the price and the arrangement worked well until he was caught again.

What he lacked in refinement as a thief he made up for in volume. When he was apprehended this time it was evident from the amount of goods found in his room that he had violated a number of premises. The police tracked down the goods with a little help from Jimmy who was gently persuaded by a huge constable and the promise that it would be worse if he didn't cooperate. He wasn't sure how that could be, but he cooperated, nevertheless.

After all the tracing and accounting was completed Jimmy was back in court where the magistrate noted his three previous convictions and that his offending seemed to be escalating. This time he faced five counts of larceny and housebreaking.

That's not too bad, thought Jimmy. *There were plenty more not listed and what about those I did when I was liquored up and can't remember anyway.*

The charges were found proven and Jimmy was sentenced to five years in a reformatory prison with hard labour. He was sent to Ballarat prison. *Nice, back in the country again. I never did like Pentridge, too big and full of the worst type of criminals.*

*

After spending some time at Ballarat, Jimmy was sent to the relatively new French Island Reformatory Prison, also known as the McLeod Training Centre, which was opened in 1916. Its aim was to be a self-supporting prison farm and keep the men away from the city and its criminal distractions. It was hoped the prison farm would instil in the prisoners some sort of work ethic so they were able rejoin the outside world when their sentence was complete. Most prisoners were low risk/ low security and the running of the prison was comparatively relaxed. The men had their own cells and were only locked in at night.

The settlement was on an island. The only access via a ferry which made the crossing to Crib Point once a day. The small local population was well known to the ferry captain and deckhands so an unescorted prisoner was easily identified and recaptured. Undoubtedly some inmates dreamed of building a boat or swimming to escape, but the distance to the mainland was too far, few of them were strong swimmers, and the water was cold and rough.

Jimmy's arrival at the island was pleasant and had him thinking it was like a holiday with himself as a tourist. Magpies carolled in the trees and as the ferry left the wharf the seagulls swooped into its wake in their search for fish. The smell of the sea air was invigorating and seemed to be good for his lungs.

After reception he was presented to the governor, a man called Corbeau. 'Ah D'Aubin, you are French,' he crowed to Jimmy. 'Do you have any skills that we can use here?'

Well, thought Jimmy, *I'm not sure.* 'I can butcher an animal,' he said. 'Excellent,' said the governor, 'you are now in charge of our butchery.'

The farm had a range of cattle, sheep, pigs and poultry which required butchering on a regular basis and there was always work to be done. Animals had to be slaughtered every day for consumption fairly quickly as there was no refrigeration. Jimmy had trouble handling the heavy work so Corbeau gave him another man to help. Jimmy liked the work and found it was quite relaxing. He didn't have to deal with customers and the food was free. The prison staff and the inmates appreciated his work and he felt he was doing something useful.

Things went well for him over the next few years with the cycle of the seasons, the men coming and going, the weather and the sea. He liked the animals and when he wasn't butchering, he helped raise them. He explained to the other men how to prepare the animals, to withhold feeding the day before a kill and how to handle them gently to lessen the stress on the animals and improve the quality of the meat. With the approval of Corbeau he obtained permission to purchase some turkeys and he was so pleased to see them arrive on the ferry. The men had built pens for them and they began breeding them. The first were ready in time for Christmas, a gesture greatly appreciated by prisoners and staff alike. The stock was maintained and added to the diet on a regular basis.

The men were mostly a pleasant bunch and prisoners and staff got on well with each other. The occasional fight and unpleasantness usually resulted in the culprits quickly being ferried back to the mainland to continue their education in higher security at 'Bluestone College'. Some of the prisoners had been farmers so they knew how to breed animals, sow crops and grow vegetables, which was helpful to the prison and many of the men felt they were doing something useful. There were also plenty of returned men in McLeod who had some regularity in their lives for the first time since the war and were being well fed, which they found to be really beneficial to their health.

Jimmy felt the best and healthiest he had been since he had returned.

*

When his sentence was completed in 1928, Jimmy was as

optimistic as he could be about his future. Governor Corbeau had arranged a job for him as a labourer when he got back to Melbourne.

The work was on a project to build a war memorial in St Kilda Rd to commemorate those who served in the Great War.

He found accommodation in a boarding house in Carlton where the landlady was happy to give him a room based on the promise of his job. He was able to walk to work or catch the tram if he needed to and he enjoyed the work knowing that it was for a good purpose.

His supervisor knew of his physical limitations so he put Jimmy in charge of a gang who were digging trenches for communications, water pipes and electrical conduits. With his battlefield experience with such tasks he found it easy work and although it was not part of his job he didn't hesitate to join in the digging where he could.

Every pay night he had a drink with his gang to celebrate the end of the working week. With the pubs closing at 6 pm they usually knocked off the first few beers there then proceeded to one of the illegal sly grog shops proliferating because early pub closing didn't meet the need for after-hours boozing.

As construction of the Shrine continued Jimmy's gang ended up doing other jobs until the work eventually ran out. By the early 1930s the building was complete and the workforce was laid off. The stock market crash of 1929 was beginning to bite and unemployment was growing. Jimmy was out of work and his savings were dwindling at the same time as his alcohol consumption was again increasing.

Due to the high level of unemployment, the Government introduced 'the Susso', more correctly known as the Sustenance Payment. The payment was only for those who had no assets and savings, and those who had been unemployed for a long time. Jimmy quickly became well qualified in this area and soon ended up on the susso. He was chucked out of the boarding house for non-payment of rent and ended up living in a humpy down by the river.

There were a several clusters of humpies dotted around the city, some made of corrugated iron and pieces of timber, some even of cardboard. There were smoky cooking fires, mosquitoes and even the odd tiger snake. Sanitation was an issue and the camps could be smelt from some distance away.

When it was hot there was shelter under the trees, when it rained everything and everyone got wet, which was particularly bad for respiratory health. Colds and influenza spread quickly between the inhabitants.

Apart from a few families with children, it was mostly single men who lived in the humpies, among them many returned men who still hadn't worked out how to fit in, were disowned, disappointed or disoriented or all of the above. The susso gave them just enough to stay alive, although there were those like Jimmy who took their sustenance in liquid form.

This sufficed for a while but ultimately Jimmy's health again declined. He ended up in hospital with pleurisy where it took him a while to recover. They fed him up and gave him treatment so that he was fit enough to go and get sick again.

72

CHAPTER 8

HARVEST

Following his time down by the river, Jimmy had been lucky enough to scrape together enough money to enable him to return to the boarding house. He was glad to be out of the weather and also to be back under the watchful eye of Mrs Greyfood.

The boarding house made a good base for his criminal activities, sleeping, a little bit of work, and drinking. His mates and those at the pub knew where he lived and when a telegram came early one morning that had been sent care of his drinking hole, Mrs Greyfood bashed on his door to wake him from his beery slumber and slipped the message through the large gap at the bottom.

The message was from Agnes, Billy's wife, and simply said, 'Come quickly'. Jimmy was living in Fitzroy but Billy lived in

Brunswick. Jimmy didn't have any money for transport so he took off on foot and limped/ran to Brunswick as quickly as he could. Agnes greeted him in tears, her wet salty hair stuck to her face. 'It's Billy,' she said.

She was in a bad way and could barely speak.

'It's Billy, he's gone ...'

'He's in the lemon tree,' she said.

'What do you mean?'

'He's in the lemon tree,' she repeated and collapsed in the doorway.

Jimmy dashed down the side of the house, an old rose bush with brittle thorns scraping his arms and making them bleed. He turned the corner into the garden and there was the lemon tree.

And there too was Billy, his body dangling and moving slightly in the breeze, slowly spinning around. He wore his old stripy pyjama bottoms, his chest and feet were bare.

Around his neck was his belt that he had fixed to a branch on the tree in his desperation.

You haven't done a great job of that, mate, thought Jimmy in a strange random moment. It looked as if Billy had jumped from a lower branch and been slowly throttled to death.

Billy and Jimmy had spent many hours under this tree emptying the big brown bottles of beer. It was very old, planted there when the house was built, and had grown wide and tall over many years. Large smooth branches formed the lower portion but Jimmy noticed the occasional ripe fruit hanging from the leafier higher branches with their nasty thorns. The tree was in flower and the scent of lemon blossom hung over the yard, such a bright, fresh contrast to the scene holding Jimmy's gaze.

He noticed the morning dew damping Billy's hair and the urine dribbling across his left foot and dripping off his big toe. In the early morning sunshine the flies had already discovered him and were doing what flies do with dead bodies. Only they seemed to be happy.

Billy was no longer the big man of earlier times. Jimmy was able to lift him to release the belt and gently lay him on the grass. The family dog came out for a look but Jimmy found his chain and tied him up.

Jimmy couldn't believe his old mate had gone like this. He wasn't sure how it should have ended for Billy but he knew this was not the right way. His mind went back to the Western Front, to the shell blasts, the wire and the mud, and at the end, the amazement that they had made it home — and then this.

While Jimmy had been getting Billy out of the tree Agnes had made it to the back door and was looking out through the fly wire. Jimmy heard a baby crying in one of the bedrooms.

Agnes opened the door slightly and ran out into the garden. She threw herself upon her dead husband on the wet grass. But Bill was already stiff and she knew she would never feel his warmth again. Nevertheless, she held him for what seemed a long time and only when she slowly drew herself away did Jimmy take her inside and make them both a cup of tea. The baby had cried itself back to sleep, not that Agnes cared at the moment. Jimmy grabbed a blanket off the bed and went out to cover Billy's body. It didn't change things much but kept the sun off his face and the flies at bay. Jimmy and Agnes finished their drinks and between the sobs worked out what to do next.

*

By now it was about 10 am and the world was well awake, so Jimmy walked up the street and found a doctor who could examine Billy and make sure he was gone, although Jimmy had no doubts; he had seen it all before. When the doctor arrived, he said Billy was definitely departed and Jimmy must let the police know as suicide was an unexpected death.

The police duly arrived, had a look around and removed the body for the coroner's pleasure. After all the essential inquiries and paperwork were completed, Billy's remains were released to the undertaker and the funeral was arranged.

Agnes had meanwhile told Jimmy what had happened. She said that the previous night Billy had been to the pub as normal and came home for tea, had a normal evening and went to bed. In the morning she woke up and Billy wasn't there. She looked for him in the house and the outside dunny. Then in the early morning light she saw the glint of his belt buckle in the sun. She didn't know what to do and sent the message to Jimmy, Billy's oldest friend.

Nights were always long for Billy and when he closed his

eyes, he saw the hell that troubled all his dreams. In daylight hours it wasn't so bad and the drink helped too. But at night he couldn't push it away; he tried to keep on the outer edges of the vortex but the black hole at the centre was too strong. On that last night he was finally consumed and the messages in his head were too strong; he knew he had to stop it. Agnes never knew and may not have understood.

After all the official notices had been lodged and various sombre men and women had knocked on the door and offered condolences — for all the good that did — there was a funeral. There was a service that spoke of Billy and the things he had done, mostly sanitised to reflect the good and minimise the other. They carried him from the hearse to put him in the ground. Amidst the headstones and the sticky clay they put him down to lie with the others in the ordered rows and covered him up quickly. There was another funeral nearby in an hour's time.

Many thought that death by one's own hand was a sin and Hell would be the reward, but the ones who knew the vortex understood and wondered if they could hold it off.

Billy's army mates said nothing and ordered drinks at the First and Last until the cash had gone, and in the morning the publican hosed the vomit off the tiles and washed the urine and cigarette butts from the footpath.

Sad duty done, the unclean disposed of, and he was ready for a new day.

CHAPTER 9

ANOTHER BASTARD

It took Jimmy a long time to get over Billy's death. And not only a lot of time but also a considerable intake of grog. Time flows and so does grog.

He was still living in the boarding house in Fitzroy and doing the odd break-in to keep himself financial. This gave him the wherewithal to maintain his social life at the River Clyde. Jimmy knew a barman there who arranged for him to do some odd jobs as he was a bit of a handyman. Sometimes it would be painting, other times it would be sweeping the floor or cleaning. The barman wasn't big on keeping records so he would sling Jimmy a few shillings or pay him in kind. Either way, Jimmy was happy with the arrangement. What could be better for a returned man who liked to drink?

One day a new barmaid appeared called Margaret. She

was a Scot who had migrated to Australia after the 'Big Show'. She came from a poor family who were essentially destitute after the war as a result of massive unemployment in Scotland and the UK in general. She wasn't particularly skilled but had looked after her sisters after their mother had died in childbirth. Her father was a band leader but there wasn't much work for him even though he travelled the length and breadth of the country.

'When you think about it, not a great career choice,' she later commented to Jimmy, adding a wry smile.

Margaret chose to come to Australia because it was closer to her brother who had migrated to New Zealand. She soon found work as a maid in Como House in Melbourne. She enjoyed working there and it was an experience she would always remember. But the work was hard and exacting and the hours were long. She had very little time off for herself and eventually sought other work.

She lived in Heidelberg and was able to get a job in the River Clyde Hotel in Carlton. Where better for a Scottish girl?

It didn't take much imagination, time or beer for Jimmy to strike up a conversation with the pretty newcomer. He was quite the gentleman sober, but unfortunately for him, his family and the wider world this was a rare and limited condition, usually preceded by a period of imprisonment or lack of funds.

Jimmy was sufficiently attracted to her to moderate his

drinking and they ended up having a lengthy chat. He talked about his Scottish background and very roughly what he had done in the war. He only mentioned the good things so it sounded like some sort of khaki travel adventure. As for his drinking and regular imprisonment for petty crimes he revealed very little. He painted himself as an odd jobs man looking for an opportunity to better himself. Despite his current rough life Jimmy was well educated and able to convince most people (excluding magistrates) of his bona fides.

Margaret was there again the next day and the one after and gradually a relationship developed.

Eventually Jimmy took a plunge and asked Margaret if she would have tea with him at a cafe in Heidelberg. To his surprise and pleasure, she said yes, and the following Saturday they met at the Banksia Cafe for dinner. They had toasted cheese sandwiches and tomato soup washed down with a cup of tea. He paid the bill with money from the pawn shop and afterwards they went for a walk. As he had hoped, Margaret invited him back to her place. Things developed pretty quickly from there and they were soon thrashing around on an old metal bed, an experience they both enjoyed to the extent that Margaret let Jimmy stay the night.

In the morning, Jimmy went home and back to work, or what passed for it. From then on he and Margaret met in the bar most days and repeated the experience with the metal bed head, which eventually punched a hole in the plaster wall due to their exertions.

A couple of months later, Jimmy was hanging over the bar as usual and noticed Margaret was in tears.

'What's the trouble, love?'

She hesitated, wiped away the tears and dropped her voice to a whisper. 'Oh Jimmy, I'm late.'

For a brief moment, he looked puzzled. Then he caught on, he realised what she meant. Words wouldn't come. *What can I say? And do?*

Margaret eventually broke a long silence. 'I want to keep it,' she said. She waited in hope for Jimmy's response but knew deep down he was a poor prospect as either a husband or father. He as good as acknowledged this to be the case when he stopped staring into his beer and raised his eyes to hers.

'That's okay by me, love, but do we have to get married as well?'

'Not if you don't want to, Jimmy. We'll manage somehow.'

The decision was made, flying in the face of the custom at the time to marry as soon as a pregnancy occurred. In some ways things were fairly simple for them as Margaret's family was overseas and Jimmy was estranged from his.

Margaret being with child didn't put an end to their nocturnal activities, especially as Jimmy was hard to refuse when he had had a few. The child was born, a boy with a covering of auburn hair who they called Hamish. Jimmy continued to live in Fitzroy and Margaret in Heidelberg. Jimmy liked the boarding house life as it was conducive to the consumption of alcohol. Margaret preferred her own place for the raising of a child, something to which Jimmy paid very little attention. This arrangement went on for a few years until Margaret again became pregnant. At this point she said she had had enough and that they must get married for the sake of the children.

There was no church wedding, instead it was the registry office with a couple of witnesses. The next baby would be no bastard.

They rented a house in Waterloo Street, Carlton, and they stayed there for many years, the rent being subsidised by the pawn shop and petty crime. Later on, when he felt like he was up to it, Jimmy repaired radios using his skills with electrics and valve radios he had learnt while overseas. All his jobs were cash in hand and everyone in the neighbourhood knew where to take their radios to get them fixed.

Their house in the slums was no palace and was eventually demolished to make way for housing that was actually suitable for humans.

The new baby, born in 1933, was a girl they named Ailsa, followed a year later by a boy called Malcolm and one year after that by a second girl, called Morag. To say it was a massive struggle to look after four children with a big drinking father grossly underestimated the challenge.

Margaret was unable to work and any money that Jimmy earned was always siphoned off for grog as a priority.

CHAPTER 10

THE HEARTH

Margaret kept the house and raised the children while Jimmy was out and about working and undertaking other activities. Like the rest of Australia, Melbourne was in the grip of the Great Depression. Carlton, and certainly the bit that they lived in, was a slum area with all the filth and decay that that entailed. It exuded an awful stench as did many of its inhabitants. What mattered were not the rules, but survival. Those living there were a seething mix of migrants, those down on their luck, the unemployed, escapees from official scrutiny and many who did not fit into the social fabric of the day.

Among them were many from overseas including British, Italians and Jews, many of them having fled to Australia before and after the war. The Carlton Football Club played a prominent and vital role in the Carlton community in the days when Victoria had twelve teams and all games were played on a Saturday. Football was very tribal and many a Carlton supporter who strayed into Collingwood was bashed, and vice versa. Carlton was known, at least informally, as the North of the Yarra Jews and the St Kilda Football Club was known as the South of the Yarra Jews.

*

It was in this cauldron that Margaret raised the children with very little help from Jimmy or anyone else. The kids went to the Faraday Street primary school, a rough seat of learning at the time, full of tough kids and where fighting was a daily pastime. Getting to school unharmed could be a challenge. During World War II the children had to carry their gas masks at all the times, which sometimes precluded getting in a good punch.

Margaret managed to provide food and clothing at a subsistence level based on scrounging, occasional contributions from Jimmy, the local house of God, St Jude's, the Salvation Army and whoever else could be persuaded to part with food, clothing or cash. There were occasional windfalls such as the time when the children were roaming the street as usual and one of them found a five-pound note. One of the girls sat on the note so no one else could see it while the boys ran to get their mother. There was never a question asked about handing the money into the police or finding its rightful owner. Margaret could put it to better use.

She grabbed the note and bought food and cheap clothing for her brood. Such windfalls didn't happen very often but when they did they made a huge difference and she made sure Jimmy didn't drink it away. Jimmy's standard response when Margaret wanted money or the kids asked him for something was to say, 'Don't beg, you're old enough to steal.'

There wasn't much of a garden at the house but Margaret planted a few cuttings, and using seeds from neighbours, put in a few plants to brighten up the house and her life.

She planted poppies, hollyhocks and foxgloves. The kids were fascinated by the foxgloves with their long tubular flowers and the fact that bees entered the tubes and buzzed around like some sort of vibrating machine. Malcolm was particularly fascinated by these creatures and pinched off the end of the foxglove with his fingers to trap the tiny vibrating beasts in a floral prison. This worked well most of the time and he captured them and picked off the flower to show the other kids or his mother. Sometimes, however, the bees broke free of their prison and stung him on the fingers causing howls of pain to rise up from the garden. On such occasions he ran inside looking for comfort from his mother . . . and after the pain subsided and the sting removed, he returned to the garden to catch more bee victims.

Jimmy was no gardener; it was just somewhere to drink long necks when it was too hot inside.

Sometimes Jimmy brought home items that he had pinched,

been given or had exchanged at the pub, but it was mostly stuff for himself or the pawn shop. One evening, however, he arrived with a pot containing a Datura plant for Margaret. She had no idea where or how he obtained it and didn't ask. She tried to keep at arm's length from his extracurricular activities. But he wouldn't have told her anyway. It was a beautiful plant with long, white trumpet flowers and a sweet and powerful fragrance that was particularly strong in the evening.

She wasn't sure why Jimmy had given it to her but assumed he was after some special favour. The truth was that, like a lot of the things that Jimmy did, he didn't really know why he did it either. Margaret nurtured the plant and kept it alive for many years in the pot. Having grown up in Scotland's chillier weather, temperate climate gardening wasn't her strong suit so she was pleased she managed to keep the plant alive.

Eventually she would have a house of her own and replant the Datura, which grew very large and prolific. She always said it was the nicest thing he had ever done for her. The Datura became important to the family to the extent that some of the children and grandchildren took cuttings of it to plant in their own gardens where it could well be flourishing a hundred years later.

*

To supplement the family income, Malcolm sold the *Melbourne Herald* on street corners in the city. The newspaper had several editions each day so there was always work available for young boys to sell it to passers-by.

It was a job Malcolm could do after school and in the evening. The downside was that it had to be done in any weather: hail, rain or shine. There wasn't much money in it but sometimes it was enough to put food on the table. The paperboys' call of '*Heraaald*' echoing across the city was a familiar Melbourne city sound. Most workers grabbed a copy on their way to work and another on the way home, with the later edition having the most up-to-date news. When extraordinary news broke, either locally or elsewhere, a 'Special' edition was published. Train carriages were full of people juggling the large broadsheet pages, which blocked out the view and rustled against non-readers' faces. The bonus for those who hadn't bought a paper was that it could be easily read over someone else's shoulder.

*

One day, Malcolm was bitten on the leg by a spider. This was not an unusual occurrence as he was an adventurous child. But this time his leg swelled up and he was unable to walk. Margaret took him to the Royal Children's Hospital for attention.

The doctors told her the bite was infected and there was no alternative but to amputate the limb. Margaret agonised about this wondering what to do as the boy was in so much pain. She decided not to let the doctors take the leg as the surgery was unlikely to save his life due to the infection. As the days went by, the infection subsided and Malcolm was released from hospital with his leg intact. Margaret's gamble paid off and the child survived. In later years when playing football, basketball and running, Malcolm was thankful for the decision his mother had made.

*

To say that times were hard would be an understatement for people and families like Margaret and Jimmy who had endured the Great War, the Great Depression and then the Second World War. There had been no respite, no chance to recover, no chance to amass savings or get on top of their situation, their health or life in general. In many ways life was something heaped on to them and they went along with it because they were incapable of changing it. They didn't know what to change or how to do it because they lacked the inspiration and resources to achieve it.

A potential escape route for Malcolm opened up unexpectedly when Jimmy's brother Boyd, and his wife Anne, began exploring whether they could adopt him. They liked the child as he was quick-thinking, intelligent and had lovely snowy hair — to them, in some ways, the perfect child.

Anne was unable to have children and adoption seemed a perfect solution. They were both keen and so was Malcolm — and of course Jimmy was all for it too.

Margaret was more hesitant. Malcolm spent occasional

weekends at Boyd's house in Kew and loved it. Everything was clean, there were toys, plenty of food, and he had his own bedroom. Boyd and Anne longed for children and they knew that they could offer him a better life, a better education, and prospects for the future. Boyd and Jimmy's parents still lived nearby in Hawthorn and Malcolm always remembered that when Margaret, he and his brother and sisters visited, they were shuffled out the backdoor when other wealthier and more presentable members of the family arrived.

Jimmy's parents certainly didn't approve of the life he lived and the way he went about it. He was far from being the much-loved child or the patriotic soldier; instead, he was a criminal and an alcoholic, and he wasn't welcome.

As preparations for the adoption proceeded, all parties seemed to be committed to the process. Margaret, however, voiced her reservations. Yes, it would be a lot easier for her family to have one less mouth to feed and make her life somewhat easier.

'No, I'll not allow it,' she told one family gathering. 'Malcolm's my son, no one else's, and that's what really matters.'

The adoption process came to an abrupt end. Malcolm mistakenly thought it was because his uncle and aunt had rejected him. On the day that the final decision was made, he clung on to the front fence as Margaret led him and his siblings away. 'You buggers, you buggers, you buggers!' he raged back at the house.

*

Jimmy and Margaret's older son, Hamish, was considered unconventional largely because of his keen interest in the theatre and the arts. He ultimately became a male model for Myer and other department stores. Hamish had numerous male friends and spent much of his time with them. When he left home he rented a room and often had male friends stay the night, causing his suspicious landlady to squeal to the police. They visited the premises and arrested Hamish, charging him with indulging in homosexual acts. He appeared in court where the charges were found proven and he was sentenced to twelve months' imprisonment in Pentridge, but not in Jimmy's old room.

*

Margaret didn't get out much as there was no money to spare and nowhere to go. By the time she had finished the cooking, cleaning and dodging Jimmy, there was no time she could call her own.

On one memorable occasion the entire family visited the Exhibition Gardens, the girls done up in their cleanest clothes, with bows in their hair, and they even posed for a photo in front of a fountain.

There was Jimmy with the kids, seemingly transported to another world, all done up in an old but clean suit, almost bald and thus looking more like their grandfather than their father.

The children appeared full of life, but their father's tortured life was written large and clear on his face.

CHAPTER 11

THE DRINKING WAR

The personal war inside Jimmy never stopped and the external evidence never told the true story. While the Great War had finished, during the 1930s another was brewing in Europe and Asia.

Again, Australia would be involved because it was what the government thought was the right thing to do.

For Jimmy, the new war would be very different from the one before. He was older and damaged, more cynical, and had no wish to be involved. Any patriotic thoughts he might have had had long since been pissed away via the booze. As long as his life could continue pretty much as it was, he would be happy.

The preparations for more killing, much of it more sophisticated and on a grander scale, provided plenty of work that paid well even for unskilled men like Jimmy. His brother Boyd, who worked for the army in designing camouflage and who was a fine citizen, was able to get him a job in a munitions factory at Maribyrnong.

He was mainly used as a handyman but occasionally also worked on the production line. The workers were mostly women plus a few older men like Jimmy as many of the able-bodied young men were away fighting overseas. The years of drinking were beginning to take their toll on his body and his hands had a slight tremor, hardly the sort of person that should be handling detonators for shells. He wasn't the only one with shaky hands and from time to time there were accidents in the factory. The more serious accidents resulted in casualties and whenever there was a big boom Jimmy inexplicably found himself on the floor under the bench and taking a while to come out.

Despite the downsides, the job paid well and Margaret was cheered to find Jimmy was unable to drink it all away. So some of it made its way into her hands to help with the rent and the raising of the children. Sometimes Jimmy handed her the spare money but other times she went through his pockets at night after he had passed out. He wasn't the greatest worker and much of his best work was done through an alcoholic haze. In normal times he would have been sacked but the factory was desperate for labour. It was also policy to look after returned men, especially those who had fallen on hard times. This was true generally in employment, so Jimmy got a good run.

He actually had a pretty good war, even if much of his time was spent intoxicated at the bar of the River Clyde. It gave him a chance to buy back some of the items that he had pawned over the years, bits and pieces that he had owned or had taken from Margaret. Proceeds of his thieving had ended up in the pawn shop in return for cash, but right now he had little need to steal because he was making good money.

Out in the street one day he heard a plane fly over, one of many to be seen in the skies at the time as pilots and aircrew were being trained for the war effort. The sound of an aero engine wasn't that unfamiliar to Jimmy but he couldn't help looking up, surprised to see red roundels under the plane's wings. It was a Japanese Mitsubishi Zero.

Sightings of the 'enemy' plane were widely reported and the Department of Defence reassuringly reported that the air force had flown it over Melbourne to see if the public had noticed it. When Jimmy's son asked him if it was a real Japanese plane and it meant Japan was about to invade Australia, Jimmy fell about laughing. He had been on ships and seen how far away Australia was from the rest of the world and he could not imagine the Japanese making it to Australia. His son did not know what to make of this as Jimmy was out of step with everyone else he spoke to.

Another Japanese seaplane was later seen over Melbourne and it was barely reported. But this one was real and had been launched from a Japanese ship in Bass Strait for reconnaissance. Although the Japanese had bombed Darwin, people in Melbourne thought there was little to fear as that was so far away.

The war may have been financially helpful for Jimmy and his family, but the greater availability of funds meant he drank more and more, barely able to get to work or get home. When the war finished, Jimmy managed to keep working for a couple more years, but shortly he ended up out on the street.

CHAPTER 12

CONTINENTAL DRIFT

Time passed. World War Two finished and Jimmy found himself out of a job as the munitions factory scaled back production to much lower levels. He spent more time working on radios and his usual social (but really antisocial) activities.

Margaret saw nothing positive in Jimmy's greater freedom from work as he spent more time around the house and indulging himself. This had an impact on her and the kids. The verbal abuse, the drinking and general obnoxiousness increased. So, too, did the beatings, which were in inverse proportion to their household income as any money Jimmy had previously provided had evaporated.

He was also getting older. That, together with his injuries and other proclivities, meant it was almost impossible for him to gain any employment. It even affected his ability to commit petty crime. Jimmy had pawned anything the family possessed that was of any value and he himself was not a net producer.

*

Margaret had had enough of making excuses for broken bones and black eyes, claiming fictional walks into doors, worrying about herself and the children. It all came to a head one night when Jimmy came home drunk as usual. He got stuck into her, breaking furniture and smashing crockery.

He had her down on the floor and was smashing her face into the table leg when their two sons, now older and stronger, heard her screams and came running down the hallway from their bedroom to help her. They had heard all this before but this time they felt they were able to help.

They jumped on their father's back, punching him and dragging him off their mother.

'Get out, leave us alone,' one of them screamed.

They pushed him out the front door and locked it so he couldn't get back inside.

There they left him to sleep it off.

*

Next morning, Margaret would only speak to Jimmy through the closed door. She didn't mince her words, spoken in subdued anger. No shouting or screaming, but quiet and very firm. 'I'm chucking you out and don't want you coming back.' And in case he didn't get her message through his befuddled brain, she added, 'I never want to see you again.'

She quickly and briefly opened the door. Only enough time to throw out Jimmy's belongings, just a few crumpled clothes and that was all.

'That's the lot, there's nothing more. Now get away from here and leave us all alone.'

Jimmy was confused and still slightly drunk from the night before. He wandered off up the street in a daze but understanding that this part of his life was over. He found some welcoming bushes in the nearby creek and slept for the rest of the day.

*

It was uncommon and shameful at the time to terminate a marriage no matter how bad it was. But Margaret wanted to finalise it and remove Jimmy from her life.

Following Jimmy's exit, Margaret was able to obtain work and the children also found employment. Margaret and her daughters worked in the Pelaco shirt factory, Hamish in fashion and Malcolm for the Postmaster General's department.

Margaret eventually gained the help of a sympathetic lawyer pro bono and lodged divorce proceedings. Her application was granted on the basis of abandonment and cruelty.

She gave her lawyer a grim half-smile. 'There was certainly plenty of that,' she said.

She set about creating a better life for her small family and in time, helped by the wages the family could now earn, was able to purchase a small house in Merlynston with space for a real garden, vegetables, fruit trees, and a sheltered spot near the house for the formerly constrained and potted Datura — which grew healthily and large in the new ground.

The plant appeared often in photos of children and grandchildren as it and the family grew.

Jimmy was on skid row and lived on the streets.

CHAPTER 13

STEEP DESCENT

Jimmy was homeless after Margaret threw him out, dossing down in the park and back alleys. He even camped among the larger monuments at Melbourne General Cemetery as they provided excellent shelter.

He used old sheds in industrial areas, back gardens and deserted factories until he was discovered and moved on. He scavenged and stole for food and, though his funds were limited, he still found ways to pay for his drinking. Picking up coins from fountains, loose change, begging, pawning stuff he had stolen all helped. The lack of cash limited his choice of drink and all he could afford were flagons of cheap red wine, or 'plonk' as it was called. But it did the trick and drowned the demons for another day until the sober dawn.

Jimmy's days began with a glimmer of hope but by

nightfall it was dashed and lubricated to ease the darkness and the loneliness that he experienced, which he could neither understand nor explain. He kept doing it day after day, week after week, month after month and year after year, all the time getting sicker and sicker and more confused.

People occasionally took pity on him and gave him an odd job for a bit of cash or a feed. Because he mainly roamed the Carlton area he knew, his children still saw him from time to time, but relationships were strained and the parties weren't sure how to speak to each other. The children didn't understand how a man, their father, could be like this, how he couldn't respond to them, how he devoted himself to the bottle and how he had extracted himself from the regular world.

They kept trying but communication was fleeting and evaporated almost instantly. Nevertheless, when their paths did cross, they would often slip their father some cash, buy him a feed, provide a food parcel or give him some new clothes. He was always in need of any of these items. Living rough was far from easy but Jimmy now knew no other way. He was always unkempt with straggly, matted, dirty hair and a beard spotted with food and other nondescript substances. The children often cut off the worst bits despite his protests, until the next time.

He lived in his filthy clothes day and night and because toileting wasn't a priority, he often wet himself and worse, and always stank of urine. There was no point in washing the ragged clothes and the best thing that could be done was to dispose of them as quickly as possible and find him some new ones. He preferred to wear suits and shirts as a lot of the older men did. Sometimes he wore underpants, but due to the frequent accidents he discarded these as often as not, leaving them where they fell for passers-by to wonder at their origin as the garments added another layer to the rubbish that decorated the streets in areas of the city frequented by the homeless men: supplements to the bottles, surreptitious turds and other grotty bric-a-brac.

Summers on the streets were hot and dry, the only shade provided by the odd tree or grimy building. The men sat on the kerbside bluestones drinking at any time of the day, necking grog from bottles in brown paper bags. They ate if they had money or found some scraps, but generally went unfed and hungry, and consequently lost weight. They became scarecrows with tight belts and strained faces. Some died from dehydration or starvation and were found curled up in a laneway corner next to the metal rubbish bins, discovered by an unfortunate garbo on his weekly rounds.

They slept on the same cobblestones where they had been sitting when that day's grog ran out, surrounded by the empties and maybe covered with a newspaper or an old coat for warmth. Those who preferred a more natural setting were sometimes lucky enough to score a park bench in the Carlton Gardens but they had to put up with brushtail possums chasing each other, rooting and squealing all night. Mostly this wasn't a problem, as their high levels of drunkenness eventually saw tortured sleep come creeping in.

Winter was cruel, bringing coughs and colds and, for Jimmy, pneumonia. His bad lungs ensured repeated bouts of respiratory illness, bronchitis, pleurisy, the lot. When he could, he tried to get a bed at a refuge for alcoholics and homeless men, like The Gill in A'Beckett Street or the like. He stayed for as long as it took for his illness to improve and then he was off again. He hated the rules and the other men; he just wanted to be left alone to drink and think or not.

On the other hand, when he had a bed, staff stripped off his clothes, gave him a shower, a fresh set of second-hand clothes and a feed. On one occasion they had to cut off his singlet when his chest and body hair had grown through the thin fabric. It was impossible to remove it any other way. They tried to discharge the men lice-free but the creatures were persistent and it didn't take them long to build up in numbers and feast on the intoxicating blood again. Shelters such as The Gill performed a useful respite service, but they wouldn't give him a drink. For an alcoholic the problem was obvious.

Sleeping on the streets gave freedom to drink but it also had dangers. In their stupor the men were at risk from passing traffic and other humans. Drunks would steal from them and take what little they had, whether money, a hat or a blanket or some other valuable possession. They might throw a few half-hearted punches or bite an ear but the injuries were usually minor. Of greater concern were other humans. Young men with a few drinks on board often spent a Saturday night going around the city bashing up drunks for fun. Jimmy had been bashed a few times, mostly receiving nothing more than a few bruises, but twice he had had the shit kicked out of him and once copped a couple of broken ribs.

All the time his physical and mental health declined.

In one of his lucid moments, he thought how his mother's words had come true. 'You drink enough grog and it addles your brain,' he remembered her once saying.

Now Jimmy's brain was truly addled and his confusion grew. When he entered The Gill one night he had a bit of a turn and an ambulance rushed him to hospital. The medics saw he was a hopeless alcoholic and the doctors had him detained and made a ward of the state.

CHAPTER 14

SUNBURY

Jimmy was transferred to the Sunbury Mental Hospital and put into a ward with similar men, most of them with alcohol problems, the major one being that they had had too much.

The general treatment was to keep the men confined and away from the liquid temptations of the outside world. Sometimes this worked and over time men recovered at least to some extent and were able to be released to continue their lives. Sometimes they were back far too soon. Other times they were found dead in bed in the morning without a mark on them or covered in fresh blood from a ruptured stomach ulcer. It was a grim place.

The hospital sat on a hill far enough out of town to not contaminate the townspeople or for them to hear the howling of the inmates at night. The only consolation for Jimmy and other patients was the great view of the town and in the other direction the city of Melbourne. How frustrating it must have been for them to see but to be so constrained. The authorities were very keen for these human animals not to escape and built a high brick wall with a ditch on the inside reminiscent of building works to contain other creatures in Parkville, home of the Melbourne Zoo.

Families could visit the hospital but Jimmy rarely received a visit from any of his children. Sunbury — for many years a lunatic asylum — was intended as a place for outcasts, where society could distance itself from some of its worst creations and secrete them away until they were buried and covered up forever.

The men were the worst of the worst. Some were zombies, bashing their heads against the walls until the white paint was stained red with blood. Others sat in chairs or were tied to them in the day room or outside in the garden, condemned to stare through the wire at a place they could never hope to go — although they probably never had such thoughts, or any others, so destroyed were their brains. Nothing but blank, non-blinking eyes that let in light and not much else.

*

Jimmy was really crazy by now but was able to hold it together in some measure for some of the time. He had permanent tremors and difficulty separating reality from imagination. At night he visualised all manner of things and was known to see enemy planes flying down the walls and Michelangelo painting the ceiling of the room. Who knows what else he saw when he was asleep? But whatever it was, it was enough to leave him sweating and screaming and calling out for help. Despite trying various medications, the doctors couldn't stop Jimmy's hallucinations.

Jimmy didn't make friends easily. Communication was difficult for all the men. They barely acknowledged each other's existence and grunted and growled when they had to. One patient whom Jimmy really hated was a man named Lothar, tall and missing his right hand. There was something about him that Jimmy detested and he always niggled him when he had the chance. One day, the orderlies found them rolling around in the dust in the garden, growling, scratching and biting chunks out of each other. The men were separated, patched up and moved to separate wards, as the supervisors did not want to see a repeat of the situation. Such fights were not unusual and there were instances where severe injuries and even death had occurred.

After the fight Jimmy felt an incredible urge to escape. He wanted to be free again, away from control and able to do whatever he wanted, even if he didn't really know what that was. Patients were sometimes granted leave if the authorities felt their condition had stabilised and they were no longer a danger to themselves and others. It was usually for a short period of time, but gradually extended with the aim being for them to reintegrate. While this was a fervent and widespread hope, a high percentage of the men found the bottle again and lubricated their way into a new chapter of confusion with all roads leading back to Sunbury.

CHAPTER 15
GOING HOME FOR CHRISTMAS

After a time, the doctors noted that Jimmy's behaviour had become noticeably better; his mental condition seemed to be more normal and had stabilised. As Christmas 1957 approached he applied for three days' trial leave which, based on the perceived improvement in his condition, was granted. He had a plan but no plan really, other than to get out and be free. He was given some money from his pension, enough for train and tram tickets, accommodation and food, knowing full well that many patients never made it any further than the Ball Court Hotel.

On Christmas Eve, Jimmy left Sunbury telling them he would be back in three days. He walked to the railway station and caught a train to Flinders Street Station, looking into backyards and gardens by the track as the train rattled by.

When the train pulled up in the city he got off and walked across the road to Young and Jackson's hotel and ordered a jug of beer and a pot glass and sat down at a table by himself. It was a hot day and he watched the beauty of the condensation on the jug form in the heat and gradually become droplets that rolled off and pooled on the table.

First pot downed, then the rest of the jug, then another jug and another. Now it was time for a sleep somewhere. Jimmy staggered out into the bright sunlight in Swanston Street, bumping into people as he zig-zagged across the footpath, taking big steps as if he was walking on the moon. He burped and farted as he went, crossing ahead of the lights, dodging cars, cops, poles and bins all the way to Carlton. He found a warm sunny spot to sleep on the grass near a garden bed and drifted off. When he woke it was nearly dark and he was nearly sober. He noticed a wet patch on the back of his jacket and he discovered it was the result of lying down on a fresh dog turd, but he was not at all concerned.

He headed for the nearest pub and repeated the jug-swilling exercise. After being thrown out for pissing himself in the bar, he found a cosy corner down an alley to sleep on the warm bluestones.

The following day was Christmas, but this meant nothing to Jimmy. He was still able to get his hands on some grog and over the next few days continued his ramble. When the money was running low, he bought cheap port. Rough, but it did the trick. Grog was not good for Jimmy but he was oblivious to its harm and gradually slid into a catatonic mental state. He hadn't eaten since he had been released from Sunbury. His body was very weak but he failed to realise it.

It had been more than three days since he went on leave and his absence had been noticed. But at Sunbury this was common. Most patients made their way back eventually, or were brought back by their families or the police. The hospital thought Jimmy would make his way back when his bender was finished.

While his absence had been noticed by others, it hadn't been noticed by Jimmy and he continued his adventure without much thought. He was so confused, with no money, dishevelled, dirty, disoriented, wandering through half-remembered places in his craziness, looking for non-existent people, mixing up timescales of his life and events. He scrabbled through the cemetery mumbling at the inscriptions, hiding in the crypts, crawling through the drains and puddles of waste water, scratched by blackberries behind back fences, scraped by wire, covered in mud, exhausted.

*

In his deluded state, Jimmy returned to the old house in Waterloo Street to discover that someone else now lived there. He was scared off when they found him trying to get through a window.

He took off up the lane, heart beating, not knowing

what to make of it. He stumbled around for the afternoon, stopping to drink out of a bird bath in the park, not minding the feathers or slimy taste.

Eventually he found his way to the gardens in Newman College at the University of Melbourne. Suddenly he felt so tired. There was a pain in his chest. He lay down on the grass on his back, blue eyes open, staring into the clear summer sky with the cicadas singing in the background.

That is how he was found, with no pulse or respiration. The police arrived and called an ambulance. He was taken to the Royal Melbourne Hospital, where he was pronounced dead at 7 pm on 9 January 1958.

Jimmy wasn't going back to Sunbury.

EPILOGUE
RETURN TO DUST

Because Jimmy was found in a public place and the cause of his death was unknown, an autopsy was performed and a coroner's inquiry was held. It was determined that Jimmy had died from atherosclerosis, and he had small pitted kidneys and severe lung damage. The coroner didn't notice anything else.

His son, Malcolm, who was required to formally identify a father he had never seen unclothed, saw the withered damaged arm, the shrapnel wounds and scars in the throat, head and groin, the scalloped bone in the leg and the missing calf muscle. He remembered the coughing in the night, the pain in his father's mind that he couldn't imagine; yes, he was sure it was his father. He never cried so much before or since; he hadn't been sure about his father's pain, but now he had more than an inkling.

On the day Jimmy joined the others out at Fawkner Cemetery, only a handful of mourners attended the service. His brothers and Malcolm remembered him in silence as the lumps of dirt bounced off the cheap coffin. The gravedigger filled in the hole and that was the end of Jimmy.

The grass slowly grew back over the disturbed ground and bull ants scurried about their business diving in and out of the cracks and climbing on the tombstones in search of prey.

To this day the resting place remains unmarked, and identifiable only on the cemetery map. The bull ants still scurry across the no-man's land among the bits of bark and faded plastic flowers blown in by the wind.

Oblivious to the world, Jimmy sleeps on.

PASSCHENDAELE 100

BY JAMES WILSON

Before my father
The other James
Left to greet the mincer with his youth
Somewhere off the Menin Road
To catch the metal with his leg and arm and head
And breathe the yellow gas
In slippery pools of mud
With bits of other men, the horses and the blasted trees
Until the stretcher came
Returning home with bandaged eyes
And guided off the ship
To seek brown bottles for the pain
With Pentridged prescriptions as required or loony bin for years
Until the summer's day
When it was finished
The final sleep with blue eyes open
Returning to the unmarked ground
Like the others left in Passchendaele.

GLOSSARY

Australian Imperial Force (AIF) — The Australian Commonwealth Military Forces

AWOL — Absent Without Leave

Bluestone College — prison, especially Pentridge Prison

Cactoblastis beetle — a small moth that was introduced to control prickly pear, which was a significant pastoral weed in the 1920s

Datura — a type of plant, also known as Angel's Trumpet

Duckboard — wooden boarded track across muddy or swampy areas

Enfilade — allowing the shooting of targets in a row

Estaminet — French hostelry usually serving meals and alcohol

Gelbkreuz (Yellow Cross) — German mustard gas shell, marked with a yellow cross

Plonk — cheap red wine

Pozzie — carved out position for a man or men in a trench wall

Traverse — earthen embankment in a trench which helped limit injury from fire

www.ingramcontent.com/pod-product-compliance
Lightning Source LLC
Chambersburg PA
CBHW030806190726
48285CB00003B/1048